To: Ku

The QPID Archives

Book one: The Secret

By

Kristi Bledsoe

Kristi Bledsoe

Garrels Publishing

To my family, who gave me the time and encouragement I needed to tell my stories.

Copyright 2008 by Kristi Doyle

All rights reserved

www.q-p-i-d.com

Prologue

Ever have one of those feelings that something just isn't right? Not necessarily in a good or bad way, just not quite right. Like when you get goose bumps in hundred-degree weather or a friend acts like a total stranger. It happens once in a while. But what if it happens a lot? You know, if you stumble once, it's a fluke. Stumble twice and it's a coincidence. But stumble a third time and you'd better check your shoelaces!

Julie Hatcher was twelve when she starting noticing lots of weird things that just didn't add up. There were too many to be simply a fluke or coincidence.

And they all involved her mother.

Chapter One

It all started on a Saturday morning. Julie was with her family at her little brother's baseball game. Ten-year-old Stuart was in the wrong spot, but it probably didn't matter since his team was losing again anyway. As Julie's attention wandered, she realized with a start that her mother, Annette, was no longer in the bleachers.

"Move over, Stuart," her father, Jack, was yelling, hands cupped around his mouth. Stuart's baseball cap was in his glove while he ran his fingers through his curly brown hair. "Stuart! You need to be over there." Jack sat back down, shaking his head and grinning at Julie. "I swear I get a dozen gray hairs with each game." He swept his hair back just like Stuart had done. It had the same curls but was half gray and half black.

"Ah, Dad. The gray just makes you look *distinguished*,"

she said. She lifted her chin and tried to sound snooty, but her wide smile ruined the effect. Her father's only response was a groan that sounded suspiciously like a chuckle.

"Where's Mom?"

"She went to get something to drink." His hand waved in the direction of the snack bar. "More, Stuart, keep going." He stood up again and motioned with his arms.

Julie shaded her blue-green eyes with her left hand and glanced at the snack bar to see if she could spot her mother. Flipping her light brown hair back over her shoulder, she smiled to herself as her gaze lit upon the junior high school. Here was the real reason she came along today. A perfect time to sneak a look inside the school she'd be going to next year.

"I'm going to the restroom, Dad."

"Sure, Jule," he replied, eyes on the game as he sat back down.

Julie clambered down the bleachers and hurried toward the junior high. She knew that Carrie, Brenna, and Sarah hadn't been inside the school yet. Maybe it would be open and *this* time, she would get to be first at something.

She slowed as she caught sight of a group of girls chattering. They were from her school but she didn't know them well. Julie tried a shy smile as she approached. She was met by blank looks. Feeling her face grow hot, she looked down at the ground and walked on by. She wished she were more like her friend Carrie who could talk to anybody.

The girls slipped from her mind as Julie reached the main doors. A triumphant "yes" escaped her lips as the handle turned and she slipped inside. Echoes from the huge gym encouraged her to look there first. Ah, basketball practice. That explains why the doors were open. She wandered the halls, concentrating on details so she could dazzle her friends during Orientation Week. Individual rooms were locked, but she had other clues to help her figure them out. She peeked through the small window of one door and saw a lot of glass display cases and a table with microscopes. Some sort of science class. Huh, that one with all the computers was a no-brainer. This room had posters of the Eiffel Tower and the Arc de Triumph. French class would be her guess.

More doors continued on past another hallway to her left. So many rooms! Hope she didn't get lost the first week. Huge windows drew her attention down the new corridor. Boring locked classrooms were forgotten when she realized she had found the library!

"Wow, look at all those books!" Julie muttered, nose almost touching the glass. Shelves and shelves of new adventures! She couldn't wait to get her hands on as many as she was allowed to check out. But not until next year.

She sighed. Better head back to the bleachers before her parents wondered why going to the bathroom took so long.

Besides, Mom should have those sodas by now.

She turned to go but a sudden movement caught her eye. Who'd be in a school library on a Saturday? She saw a man inside just coming into view from between two bookshelves. He had white hair but didn't look that old. The man halted by a stack of books, and turned to speak to someone following him.

Julie gasped. Mom! What was she doing here? Who was that man? She pressed her ear to the window but could only make out a faint murmur. It couldn't be a teacher; her family didn't know anyone at this school yet. Maybe another parent? But how could her mother just run into somebody in the library? This was nowhere near the snack bar! What was going on?

The man handed a small card to her mother, and they shook hands. Both started for the library exit so Julie ducked below the window and hurried away. She heard the door open as she rounded the corner. Julie ran. She did *not* want to get caught spying on her mother!

Julie made a beeline for the bleachers, with quick glances over her shoulder to see if her mother had come out yet. She plopped down next to her father only slightly out of breath. Good! Mom hadn't even left the building yet!

Who was that guy? Maybe Dad knew about Mom meeting someone and he just didn't mention it. Julie shook her head. This was silly. That guy was probably just someone her mother knew from a volunteer activity. When she came back, she would probably tell them all about it.

"Sodas all around!" Julie nearly jumped out of her skin. Her mother was climbing up the bleachers, carefully balancing three cups. How did she get here so fast? I would have seen her! Julie took the offered drink. Her heart pounded in her ears. She couldn't think clearly! Maybe her mother came out a different door that Julie hadn't noticed.

Her mother sat down and turned to Jack. "How's Stuart doing?"

Julie felt her jaw drop. What about the unknown man? Why didn't her mother say anything about meeting someone? Was she hiding something? Julie couldn't ask or she would have to confess that she'd been spying. Her stomach tightened, but she tried to ignore it and told herself to be reasonable. People often said that she had an overactive imagination. Her mother must have run into a parent or teacher, and it just wasn't important enough to mention. Her mother wouldn't lie. Would she?

Chapter Two

It took about a month before Julie managed to quit thinking about the library incident. But then other strange stuff started happening.

"Julie, Stuart! Who wants to go shopping with me this morning?" Annette called up the stairs.

Stuart's head popped out of his doorway. "Remember, Mom. Dad's taking me to get a haircut," he hollered. He looked at Julie and wiped his hand across his forehead. His hazel eyes twinkled.

"Whew! Got out of that!" He flashed a grin and disappeared back into his room. Julie heard footsteps coming up the stairs.

"How about you, Julie?" Her mother poked her head into Julie's room. "You can ask Carrie to come. I know she loves the mall."

"Sure, sounds great." She shoved her math book to the side with a sigh of relief. Shopping was a great excuse to avoid doing homework on dreaded *Math*.

"Can I ask Brenna and Sarah, too?"

"Well, I suppose since Stu's not going, it'll be fine."

Half an hour later, they arrived at Carrie's house. Brenna was already there since she lived only three houses from Carrie.

"Oh, look," her mother said as the two girls waved and ran toward the car. "Carrie cut her hair!" She winked at Julie.

Julie grinned back. "First sign of summer!" Carrie's light brown hair took on a slight curl when it was cut short. It looked like it took hours to style. Julie sighed. Carrie always managed to look elegant and spotless with very little effort. Julie often thought that if she and Carrie bought the same shirt and wore them the next day, Carrie's would actually look better than it did at the store. Julie's shirt would look like it had been washed a dozen times and slept in.

"Where's Sarah?" asked Brenna, black hair up in her usual bouncy ponytail as she climbed into the back seat. She was wearing a new Cubs jersey, one step closer to her goal of collecting a shirt from each Major League baseball team.

"You know Sarah," replied Julie. "Choir over shopping every time."

"I guess it *is* the last Saturday for choir practice before sixth-grade graduation!" remarked Carrie. All the way to the mall the girls chattered happily about what they were going to do over the summer.

After only the third store, Julie saw her mother check her watch. *That's about the fifth time she's done that*, thought Julie. After about an hour and six more watch-checks, Julie's mother said she needed to get some errands done.

"Want us to go with you, Mom?" asked Julie.

"No, you'll just get bored. Stay together, all of you, and I'll meet you right back here at a quarter to twelve so we can go to lunch. Can I trust you three to do that?"

Carrie and Brenna nodded enthusiastically, but for some reason, the scene of her mother and the strange man in the library flashed into Julie's head. She couldn't help wondering what it was that her mother had to do. Deep in thought, Julie absently followed her friends.

As the three friends came out of a clothing store, Julie did a double take. An old woman was wearing a shirt exactly like one her mother had been wearing today, white with tiny pink flowers. Up until this moment, she'd wanted to borrow the shirt from her mother. But this lady looked as old as Grandma! Whew, thought Julie. Glad I didn't borrow that! Imagine, wearing an old-lady shirt! Her friends would never let her live it down.

Two stores later, Julie spotted the old woman again.

Strange. She'd swear those pants were exactly like the ones her mother was wearing today. Her curiosity was piqued and she couldn't stop looking at the old lady. The woman turned the corner and Julie pulled her friends along.

"Hey!" said Carrie. "I want to look at those earrings!"

Julie hesitated, suddenly aware that she was acting a bit funny, following an old woman just because she was dressed like her mother. She didn't want to tell her friends about it; they would think she was weird.

"Sorry," she said, but Carrie had already moved on.

Maybe she should just forget about it. But that feeling that something was not quite right was stronger than ever.

"Look, a shoe store!" said Carrie. "I need new shoes for my graduation dress."

"I do need soccer shoes," said Brenna.

Julie rolled her eyes. "You always need some kind of sport shoe!" When they turned the corner, Julie spotted the old woman only a few yards away, talking to a petite woman with red hair, wearing a blue t-shirt and jeans. Julie deliberately looked away. Ignore her, she told herself, clenching her teeth.

Despite her determination, she kept glancing at the woman. The way she gestured, the tilt of her head. It seemed… familiar. The old woman rummaged in her handbag for paper, wrote something down and passed it to the other woman. They parted, waving to each other.

Julie stood at the entrance of the shoe store and watched the old lady enter a restroom. A strange prickling started on the back of Julie's neck. She rubbed her neck and tried to shake off the feeling.

Carrie and Brenna ducked into another jewelry store without checking to see if Julie was with them. Julie's eyes flicked back and forth between her friends and the restroom door. Two women came out but no others went in. Julie saw Carrie buy some earrings as Brenna made her way out. Julie made one more attempt at tearing her thoughts away from the old lady. She told herself it was just her imagination, but couldn't make herself believe that.

"All done," said Carrie, stuffing the package into her purse.

"Ready to go?" asked Brenna. "We have to meet your mom in about five minutes."

Julie made a sudden decision. "I've got to go to the bathroom."

"But we'll be late!" the other two said in unison.

"I'll be quick. Come on, let's go."

She hurried over to the door. She reached for the handle and nearly collided with someone coming out. All she saw was tiny pink flowers on a white background. She looked up, expecting to see gray hair. She was wrong.

"Oops! Excuse…oh, Julie!" Her mother smiled at all of them. Julie's mouth dropped open and her mind went numb.

"Well, hello girls! Isn't this lucky? Shall we go have lunch?"

"I, um, I have to go…" Julie pointed.

"All right, we'll wait."

She went in quickly, but saw no one else. She opened every stall and even looked for another exit. She found nothing to explain where the old lady had gone or how her mom got in without Julie noticing.

She left, but that prickly feeling was almost a constant itch now.

"Mom, did you see…" Rubbing her neck, Julie glanced at her friends. They just looked at her with puzzled expressions.

"See what, Julie?" But Julie found herself again remembering that strange day at the baseball game. Something peculiar was going on but what evidence did she have? Neck prickles?

"Nothing, Mom."

Chapter Three

The rest of summer was mostly normal. Julie started to think that she was just imagining things. She did her best to ignore those pesky tingles on the back of her neck, but they wouldn't stay away.

"Mom, Stuart won't get out of the bathroom." Julie swung into her mother's bedroom. Her mother slammed shut her laptop and looked up.

"Oh, Jule. You startled me." She slipped the laptop into a desk drawer. "I'll tell him he has three more minutes." As her mother walked out, those tingles started up again. Her mother used that computer for her job as an accountant, but she had never been secretive about it before.

In the two weeks that followed, Julie noticed that twice more her mother did the same thing. But four other times, she just left the laptop open and Julie could see accounting figures on the screen. Whatever she was hiding, it had nothing to do with work.

One afternoon, Julie sat on the couch, hardly noticing the television blaring something about cleaning products. She was wrapped up with thoughts of a how she could sneak a look at her mother's laptop. The phone rang in the den. Her schemes interrupted, Julie got off the couch and dashed to answer it.

"Hello?"

"Hello, may I speak with Amanda, please?"

"There's no one here by that name."

"Oh, sorry."

Julie hung up the phone, a small frown on her face. She was sure that was the same woman who left a message on the answering machine a couple of days ago. Prickle, prickle. She rubbed her neck fiercely.

"Who's on the phone?" asked her mother as she came down the stairs.

"Wrong number, looking for an Amanda."

"Oh." Her mother paused mid-step. The phone rang again and her mother turned and hurried back upstairs. "I'll get it," she said.

Julie followed to see if it was the same woman again but the bedroom door was closed. She went back downstairs and picked up the extension as quietly as she could. Instead of voices, all Julie could hear was static. She hung up. Had the phone broken within the single minute between calls? She had her answer an hour later.

"Mom, what's for dinn...oops." Her mother was on the downstairs phone. Julie backed up around the corner. She hadn't heard it ring so her mother must have called whomever she was talking to.

"Thanks, Fred. I'll talk to you later."

Who was Fred? That guy at the library? Julie heard the phone being hung up so she made a mad dash to flop on the couch. As her mother came into the room, Julie played with a lock of hair, trying to look casual. *Not* rubbing the back of her neck.

"What did you say, Julie?"

"Just wondering what was for dinner."

"Heading in there now to make spaghetti."

As soon as her mother was out of sight, Julie tiptoed back into the den. She picked up the phone. Hm, not one crackle of static. She hit redial and, after a moment, a man's voice answered.

"Weiss Cabinets. Can I help you?"

She hung up. The neck prickles turned into a chill down her back.

That night, Julie woke up around eleven o'clock desperately needing a drink of water.

"Mom must've put too much salt in the spaghetti

sauce," she grumbled to herself. As she stumbled down the hall, she noticed light coming from her parents' bedroom. The door was ajar an inch and Julie stopped when she heard her mother's voice say the name, "Fred." Julie held her breath so she wouldn't miss a word.

"Jack, the assignment will be finished soon, definitely before vacation." Oh, thought Julie. They were just talking about work and the trip to California they were taking in a month. But her feet refused to move when she heard her father's reply.

"That blasted organization is nothing but trouble. At least you get paid with your accounting job. I never was happy with all the secrets and that… that *other* stuff." Julie eyes widened. Secrets? Organization? And what is 'Other Stuff?' Goosebumps raced up and down her arms.

"Don't worry. I've never let it get in the way of our lives before and I won't now. You know I can't just leave it. I have a duty, just like my mother and grandmother."

"I know, I know. You're right. You usually finish when you say you will. Just wrap it up before vacation and we won't mention it again. Come on, Annette, put away that laptop. It's bedtime."

Julie tiptoed back to her room, thirst forgotten. Just what was Mom into? And Dad knew all about it! So what *was* going on? She had to find out. She had to know.

The answers came at the end of July.

Chapter Four

Carrie celebrated her twelfth birthday with a sleepover. As Julie leapt out of the car, she smacked her palm to her forehead and turned to her father.

"Oh, I forgot, Dad. Mom said she wouldn't get home from work until about ten o'clock and there's frozen lasagna for you and Stuart."

Her father flashed a smile and winked at Stuart in the back seat. "We'll manage!"

Julie ran up to Carrie's front door, but it was jerked open before she could knock.

"You're just in time, Julie," said Brenna. "Carrie's mom and dad are taking us to Pizza and Prizes!" She grabbed Julie's backpack and sleeping bag and tossed it all in the house. Six other girls poured from the house and piled into the van ahead of them. They all talked excitedly about which games they were going to play.

"Come on, Jule. Hurry up and finish eating," said Sarah. She was dressed up as usual, her blue party dress matching her eyes. It went perfectly with her nearly snow-white hair and pale complexion.

"Go ahead with the others; I'll just be a minute." Julie gobbled the last of her pizza and grabbed her soda to wash it down. She glanced out the window as she stood up and froze, her glass halfway to her lips. There was her mother, weaving between cars in the parking lot. She walked past the pizza parlor and went into a gift shop next door. Games forgotten, Julie's feet carried her outside, the bite of pizza going down with difficulty. It can't be Mom. She's working late at her office! Julie peered in through the gift shop windows and spotted her mother almost instantly. Curious, Julie started forward, intending to enter the store. She hesitated when her mother turned to talk to the man beside her. It was the same man that had been in the school library!

Julie's feet were rooted to the sidewalk, mouth hanging open.

"Excuse me, Miss. You can't take that outside."

"Huh? What?" A young man from the pizza place was pointing to her hand.

"That glass. You need to bring it back in."

"Um, I was just... I mean, I thought I saw someone I knew and . . . I'm sorry." Julie stared at the glass, not really seeing it as she returned to the pizza place. Suddenly, she clenched her jaw. *I'm tired of wondering what is going on,* she thought. *I'm going to get some answers!*

She slammed the glass down on the table and headed back out the door. She spotted her mother just before she turned a far corner. Julie ran as fast as she could to catch up, triumph surging through her. Julie knew that breezeway her mother had just entered was blocked off with a permanent gate. Now Mom would *have* to explain why she was not at work.

Julie rounded the corner and drew a breath to ask a question, but it caught in her throat. There was no one in the breezeway! Prickles again, with a large number of goose bumps for good measure.

"Mom?" she gasped out. The single word echoed off bare walls. There weren't any doors or exits or even anything to hide behind. Julie dashed back to the parking lot but saw only cars, none of them her mother's.

Thoughts raced around inside her brain as she returned to the pizza parlor. She tried to fit this latest mystery with all the other strange things she had witnessed, but she could not come up with a logical explanation.

"Where've you been, Julie?" Carrie grabbed her hand. "Brenna's going for the high score. Come on!"

Tomorrow, Julie promised herself. When she got home, she would do whatever it took to find answers.

****

That night at Carrie's, Julie lay awake in her sleeping bag, trying to figure out what she was going to say to her mother. One thing was sure; this was definitely not her imagination. It was deliberate deception. Her mother had lied about being at work. Julie didn't even want to think about her disappearance into thin air or the prickles might return.

"Psst!" Julie nearly jumped out of her skin. She thought all the other girls were asleep.

"Psst! Julie, are you awake?" She felt a tap on her left shoulder.

"I'm awake, Carrie," she whispered back. "What do you want?"

"What's wrong? You've been quiet all night, you hardly played any games and you didn't even finish your cake though I know chocolate is your favorite."

Julie sighed. She had a lot of friends but Carrie was her absolute best friend. They'd been inseparable since their first week in second grade. She wasn't sure why she hadn't told Carrie about all the strange stuff. But now, she had to tell someone and maybe Carrie would be able to help figure it all out. Julie opened her mouth but could get no sound out.

"Julie? Hello?" Carrie tapped her shoulder a little harder.

"I … I…" She literally could not form any words. It felt like something was stopping the words in her throat.

"Are you okay?"

"I ..." Her last attempt turned into a cough and completely different words just came out. "I just don't feel well, that's all." Julie had no idea where *that* came from.

"You sure?"

"Yeah."

"Well, don't give me what you've got! I've got a riding lesson tomorrow and I can't afford to be sick!" With that, Carrie flopped back down and rolled over.

Julie felt a chill wash down her back again. I *will* tell her, she thought. I will, I will! But strangely enough the words never came, and she fell asleep.

Chapter Five

Carrie's mother drove each of the girls home the next morning right after breakfast. Julie, groggy from lack of sleep, hadn't come up with any answers. What now? Should she confront her mother? Would Mom deny everything? And what exactly would she ask? "Hey, Mom. Been invisible lately? Met any strange guys? Lend old ladies your clothes?" Yeah, right. Her mom would send her to a shrink!

"Mom, I'm home," she yelled. She put her sleeping bag in the hall closet.

"I'm working!" came the reply from upstairs. Julie pounded up the stairs and tossed her overnight bag on her bed as she passed by on her way to her mother's room. She clenched her hands and took a deep breath, trying not to lose her nerve. She had to know!

"Hey, let a guy sleep!" Stuart shuffled out toward the

bathroom, rubbing his eyes, hair tousled. Julie's mother tipped her chair back to smile out the door at her daughter.

"How was the party?"

"Fine."

"You just missed your father by about twenty minutes."

"What? He usually goes to work about six."

Her mother lowered her voice. "I think Stu and Dad stayed up late watching a movie and ordered takeout for dinner. Mexican food by the looks of the containers in the trash." With a grin she turned back to her computer and began typing, *not* hiding what was on the screen. Julie dragged her feet over to her parents' bed and sat, elbows on her knees, resting her chin in her hands. What would she say? She didn't even know where to start.

"Mom, something's wrong with the toilet again," hollered Stuart from the bathroom down the hall. Her mother groaned and went out of the bedroom mumbling something about useless overpaid plumbers. What a stroke of luck! Julie quickly slid into the desk chair in front of the laptop. It showed accounting figures. Without really knowing why, she ignored what was on the screen, and went online instead.

Hm. Nothing out of the ordinary. She scanned previous web addresses. Wait, what was that one? Q-P-I-D? She clicked on it, glancing at the door and hoping the toilet would back up severely this time.

"Come on, log on!" The screen went blank for a second, and then a cursor appeared with a beep and a demand for a password. Julie tried everything she could think of, Mom's birthday, anniversary, but nothing worked.

"What are you doing?" Julie jumped at her mother's shout. She took a deep breath and plunged ahead.

"That's what I want to ask you, Mom." She pointed at the computer and her mother gasped when she saw what was on the screen. She lunged for her laptop, grabbing it off the desk.

"How dare you go through my personal things!" Her eyes flashed and Julie shrank back a little. She'd never seen her mother so angry. But she couldn't stop now or she'd never find out anything.

"For dinner last night, we went to Pizza and Prizes on Main and Fifth." She crossed her arms and kept a close eye on her mother.

"Oh?" Her mother looked away and, with a touch, cleared the laptop screen. The anger seemed to drain out of her. Julie knew her mother well enough to see that she was thinking hard. Her mother carefully set the computer back on the desk, eyes glued to the screen. "Sounds fun," she commented.

"Not really," replied Julie. She held her breath as her mother looked toward the door. "We went about six-thirty." Her mother finally looked at Julie and they locked eyes. The silence grew heavy and Julie could take it no longer.

"I saw you! You were supposed to be working but I saw you go in the store. Who's the guy?" Her mother opened her mouth as if to say something, but Julie kept right on talking. She couldn't keep the words from tumbling out. "Don't tell me he's a client or something. I saw him at the baseball game, too." She had the brief satisfaction of her seeing her mother's eyes widen in surprise. "What's going on, Mom?"

Julie held her breath, desperately wanting an answer but also a bit afraid. Her mother looked down at her hands then slowly reached to shut off the computer. She turned to Julie.

"I was going to wait until you were older, but I suppose I need to tell you now." As Julie half expected, her mother went to shut the door. But when she locked it as well, breakfast suddenly turned to lead in Julie's stomach.

"I want to make sure Stu doesn't walk in," she said as she sat down on the bed, eyes looking everywhere but at her daughter. She took a deep breath.

"Julie," she finally said. "You're going into junior high now, growing up." She hesitated.

"Yeeeesss," Julie said slowly, letting out the breath she'd been holding.

"What do you think about, um, relationships?"

Julie blinked at the sudden change of topics. "Relationships? You mean between boys and girls? Dating and marriage and that sort of stuff?" She gasped. "You mean you and that guy…" She couldn't go on around the sudden lump in her throat.

"No, no, no, no!" Her mother gripped Julie's shoulders and looked her straight in the eyes. "That man is only a friend. You must believe I would never do such a thing to your father or you and Stu."

Tears of relief sprang to Julie's eyes but she fought them back.

"Do you believe me?" her mother gave her shoulders a little shake. "You have to believe me."

"I don't know what to think." She clenched her fists and spoke through gritted teeth. "Why the secrecy? What are you hiding?"

"I can see why you thought what you did, but that man is a friend. We've been discussing some things about… I mean…it's something I've been working on, like a project." Her mother sighed and rubbed her forehead. "Boy, your grandmother was right; this is a lot harder than I thought it would be. Let me try another way. Do you know what a matchmaker is?"

"Sure, it's where someone matches a guy and a girl to get married." A feeling of horror crept over Julie as another possibility occurred to her. Her eyes widened as her hand went to her throat. All she could manage was a hoarse whisper. "You mean you set me up to marry someone?"

Unexpectedly, her mother burst out laughing. Julie just sat there, unable to form even one clear thought.

"I'm sorry for laughing, Jule," her mother said, wiping her eyes. "The look on your face; I've panicked you, haven't I?" Julie nodded and grinned half-heartedly, relaxing a little. It *had* been a ridiculous notion. "Let me start again. Rein in that imagination and don't jump to any conclusions. Just listen, okay?"

"Okay."

"You know I have a job as an accountant. Well, I sort of have another secret job as a kind of matchmaker. It runs in the family. Your grandmother was one and so were her mother and grandmother. I am not sure how far back it goes. Part of my current assignment is that man, Fred Weiss."

"Weiss Cabinets!" It just slipped out. Her mother's eyes narrowed.

"Just how do you know *that*?"

Julie felt her cheeks grow warm as she tried to stammer an explanation.

"I think you had better tell me everything you know." Eyes downcast, she told her mother about seeing the two in the library, and how she hit the redial to find out who her mother had been talking to.

"And then there was the woman who called for someone named Amanda, twice, and you actually talked to her even though…" She trailed off as she noticed the look of disbelief on her mother's face. Then, unexpectedly, her mother began to chuckle.

"Either I'm getting sloppy or you are very good at this sort of thing." She looked at Julie, cocking her head to one side. "Have you told anyone about any of this?"

"No. I tried telling Carrie but for some reason I couldn't." Her mother nodded as if this was expected then put her hands on her hips.

"Well! I was going to wait until you were fifteen or sixteen, but I suppose now that the secret is out, I might as well ask you now. How would you like to join the family business?"

Chapter Six

"Family business? Of matchmaking?" Julie's voice squeaked. "But I'm only twelve! How can I set people up to be married?"

"There is more to this than marriages," said her mother. "We, the agents, that is, usually just set up people to meet who normally wouldn't, and the relationship will continue from there. Agents also introduce friends, possible future co-workers and lots of situations. You see, even though most relationships between people your age won't last, they are important in helping shape who we are and how we get along with others. You won't always know the reason behind what you do but, believe me, there is one."

"How do you know who to get together?"

"Ah, let me show you." Her mother sat down at the desk and turned on her laptop again. "Now, I go to this site 'Q-P-I-D'. Make sure you have the dashes or you won't get the correct site."

She raised her eyebrow and pursed her lips as she looked sidelong at her daughter. "But you've already discovered that." Julie felt her face reddening again but was relieved to note that her mother seemed more amused than angry.

"I'll type in my access code, and…" Julie grabbed a chair for herself and dragged it over next to her mother.

"Here we are, my latest assignment." Sure enough, there on the screen was a picture of Fred Weiss with some information about him underneath. Below that was a picture of a woman who looked familiar, but before Julie could remember where she had seen her, her mother scrolled down. In flashing red letters was the phrase "Assignment completed!"

"Finished yesterday," her mother said, a proud smile on her face. "Laura is getting new cabinets in her kitchen so I gave her the number for Fred's company. However, that wasn't enough so I managed to convince Fred to help her personally because Laura has not had good luck with previous home improvements."

"Wow," was all Julie could think to say. Her mother continued to the bottom of the screen and Julie leaned close to read what was displayed. "It says you don't have another assignment yet."

"It usually takes a few weeks for another posting."

"Then how can you show me what all this is about?"

"Let's see if I can ask for one." Her mother typed in the

request. After only a few seconds the answer popped up and her mother read aloud. "'No current assignments available in your area.' I suppose we'll have to wait."

Julie suddenly remembered that her mother had gone on some business trips in the past. "Have you ever traveled for an assignment?"

"Oh, not that often. In fact, I've only done a couple of jobs away from home. One was in Oregon while I was visiting your Grandma and once during an accounting conference. Both just routine, nothing spectacular." She looked at Julie. "Why?"

"I just thought that this weekend we're going on vacation. Maybe there might be an assignment we could do near Oceanica Island."

Her mother shrugged and began typing. "Can't hurt to try." This time the response to the request was a question: "Reason for request?" Grinning, her mother typed back "Recruitment," but her smile turned to surprise when the reply read "Recruitment for Julie Hatcher?"

Julie felt a shiver run down her back. How did they know? Even her mother was giving her an odd look. But her mother entered "yes" to the question and the computer gave a small 'ping' and a phrase appeared on the screen.

"Request granted. New assignment to be posted tomorrow."

Julie put a hand to her head, suddenly feeling

overwhelmed. Her mother reached over and patted her on the knee.

"It's been a hectic morning. Why don't you take a break? I need to get back to work anyway and Stuart is going to start to wonder what's going on in here!" Numbly, Julie nodded and unlocked the door. As she was walking out, her mother called her name. "Remember." She put her finger to her lips.

Julie went to her room to lie on her bed, feeling as if her wits were scrambled. She had a vivid imagination but how in the world could she have seen this coming? Her mother, a secret agent all these years! And for some mysterious organization called QPID. Julie tried to organize her thoughts, but the lack of sleep and all the craziness of the morning caught up with her. Her last conscious thought was the realization that her mother had actually revealed very little.

"She's asleep, Mom." Stuart's voice jolted Julie out of a dream where she was matching people up according to the color of their socks and whether or not they liked chewing gum. She shook her head to dispel the rest of the vivid dream.

"She's awake now." Stuart stood right outside her door, yelling his report. No doubt getting even with Julie for waking him up this morning. He turned his head back to Julie.

"Mom says last chance for lunch." As he disappeared back down the stairs, she rolled over and looked at her clock.

Two o'clock! She leapt out of bed and hurried down to eat lunch, eager to ask questions about QPID now that her head was clear.

"Feel better?" her mother asked as she entered the kitchen. She nodded and sat down at the table. Her mother slid a ham and cheese sandwich in front of her. "Don't know why they call it a sleepover," her mother commented as she poured some milk. "Girls never get much sleep at those things." Julie had just taken a big bite when her mother turned to go.

"Mom, wait," she managed to get out around bread and meat. Her mother paused and held up her hand to keep her from saying anything else.

"Later," she whispered. Her head tilted toward Stuart who was watching television in the living room.

Julie wolfed down her lunch, managing not to choke. She was determined to find out more, but just as she put her dishes in the sink, her father came home.

"I've got baseball tickets." He waved them over his head. "Game starts in ninety minutes, let's go!" Julie heaved a frustrated sigh, knowing that the family wouldn't get home until late. Tomorrow, she promised herself.

Chapter Seven

Julie was up with the sun and done with breakfast in record time. Even so, her father had already left for work and her mother was on the computer. She motioned for Julie to close the door as she came in.

"Excited?" her mother asked as Julie pulled the chair over again.

"Yes!"

"Me, too." Her mother logged on and the new assignment flashed on the screen almost immediately. Lots of material scrolled past and both had to scan it all quickly. Two pictures were on the screen with information underneath each. One picture was of a dark-haired woman standing with twin toddler boys with the same hair and dark eyes. The other photograph showed a tall, blond man holding hands with a little girl wearing pigtails. The woman was Miranda Alvarez, twenty-nine years old. Her husband had died over a year ago. The man, Alan Hoskin, was recently divorced and had his five-year old daughter, Alicia, for the weekend.

"Do you know them?" asked Julie.

"No, but that's often the case. I usually meet one and then, well, you'll see." She requested more details on the mother of twins. Julie's eyes boggled at the information that scrolled past. She read some of it out loud.

"'First big outing with the twins. Going to Venture World this weekend. Will be in front of the barrel ride at twelve-thirty on Saturday the fifth!' Mom, that's in three days!" She looked at her mother, back at the screen, then her mother again. "How do they know all that?"

Her mother became very serious. "We are told not to ask that question."

"But…but…" She was shaken. "It…it's impossible!"

"Julie." Her mother caught her hand and squeezed it gently. The unexpected pressure broke Julie out of her shock. She looked into her mother's concerned eyes. "This is one of the Benefits of having this job, knowledge and information, and in more than just assignments. You must never abuse this or any other privilege or you will be banned from the organization forever. Also remember, you must keep all this a secret."

"Why?"

"Think how people would feel if they knew they were

'set-up' by some strange agency. They would probably fight the choices made for them."

"But who makes those choices?"

Her mother shrugged. "I've always thought of it as some higher authority. Someone who knows that certain people have to meet. So… things can come out right."

"Things? What things?"

"I don't know. Events, people. Things that will change their future for the better."

Julie snorted and shook her head. "That's ridiculous! It almost sounds like magic!"

Her mother just smiled and the prickles on the back of Julie's neck started again. Trying to ignore them, Julie searched for something to say.

"You said that information was one of the benefits. What's another? Do you get paid?"

"No, we don't get any money."

"None? You do all that work for nothing?"

"Most of the benefits are somewhat…er … less obvious."

"Like what?"

Her mother was silent for a moment. She gave a single, decisive nod. "It's easier to show you than tell you. Take my hands."

She slowly grasped her mother's hands, curious.

"Now, close your eyes. This can be disorienting at

first." Julie was confused, but she obeyed.

"Hold tight and don't let go." For about two minutes, the only thing Julie could hear was her own breathing and pounding heart. The neck prickles were slowly moving into her stomach. Something big was about to happen, she just knew it. She jumped when her mother said, "Okay, open your eyes."

Still holding hands, she looked. Sitting in front of her was a completely different woman.

"Aunt Sally!" The woman winked. Julie hesitated. But, she hadn't let go of her mom's hands, or had she? "Mom?" she whispered.

The woman she saw as her Aunt Sally nodded. "It's me. This Benefit of Disguise is one of the perks that come with the job. Sometimes a necessity."

Julie's mouth opened and closed, no sound coming out. It *was* magic! Those nervous tingles had set up camp permanently now.

"Well?" her mother asked. Julie noticed that although her mother's face had changed, her clothes hadn't. She had a sudden burst of insight.

"That day at the mall!" Her mother paled and snatched her hands out of Julie's.

"What do you mean?" she asked.

"I saw that old lady wearing your clothes! She went into the ladies' room and you came out! Was that you the whole time? The woman you spoke with, was she a client? Of course! Yesterday, your assignment! That was Laura!" She pointed at her mother then the laptop. "That's why her picture looked so familiar!"

Her mother shook her head. "It's a good thing you will be joining the agency. I think it would be impossible to hide anything from you at this point." It was a bit spooky hearing her mother's voice come from Aunt Sally's mouth. "However," she grew serious. "From now on, you had better tell me anything else you see like that. Understand?"

She watched as her mother slowly changed back. The hair was first, the same light color of brown but it actually got longer since Aunt Sally had shorter hair. Eyes were next, although blue to green was not that different. Her mother's cheeks seem to widen a little and her chin rounded just a bit. Soon she was looking at her own mother again. She had always known her aunt looked a lot like her mom, but now another thought occurred to her.

"So, I don't really have an Aunt Sally?"

Her mother laughed and ruffled Julie's hair. "Of course you do! I just picked her to look like because it's easy. I sometimes look like her, but I usually disguise myself as a stranger, so it isn't always me who sets people up. I don't want to get the reputation of being a matchmaker or I might not be as successful. It also helps to keep people from figuring out the secret. You'll understand more with each assignment."

Julie thought hard and remembered how her mother had disappeared by the pizza place.

"Is there a Teleport or Invisibility Benefit or something like that?"

Her mother's mouth dropped open. "How did you…" Julie bit her lip then told about the day at the baseball game and breezeway near the pizza place. Her mother nodded.

"That was the Benefit of Teleportation. I only had it for this assignment."

"Will I be doing that stuff?" she asked.

"Not at first," her mother replied, composure restored. "You'll be given simple assignments, appropriate to your age and beginner status. As you improve, your assignments will get more complicated. Benefits are added as they are needed."

"More complicated?"

"Sure, the better you are, the harder your assignments will be." Her mother sat up taller. "I'm proud to say that I am pretty good at what I do, and I've had some tough ones."

"But how do *they* know?" Julie waved at the computer.

"They know."

"What if I can't do it?"

"That's okay. You can change your mind at any time. Just don't let out the secret." She squeezed her daughter's shoulder. "You'll do fine. You come from a long line of matchmakers and I'll always be there to help. Now would you like to help me with this latest assignment?"

"But we're going to Oceanica Island and this one's at Venture World, isn't it?"

"There must not be any assignments where we are going, so this is evidently the best one for us." She pursed her lips. "We can probably arrange it so that we go to Venture World and Dad and Stuart still go to Oceanica Island." She looked at Julie. "Unless you'd rather not, but that would mean waiting longer for another assignment, probably a month or so."

Julie considered. She really wanted to go to Oceanica Island but she'd be crazy to pass this up. This was magic, real magic! Besides, she would die of curiosity if she had to wait for another assignment. Her mother seemed to know the answer before Julie did.

"Venture World?"

"Yeah!"

"Let's get started!"

Getting started meant lots of time with background information. To Julie's surprise, her mother spent most of the day researching only the divorced father.

"Why not both?" she asked.

"Don't really need it." Her mother smiled slyly, looking sideways at her. She scrolled down a list of people that the client Alan knew in college. Beside each name was a brief paragraph about that person as Alan had known them and what they were doing now. Julie shook her head in amazement at the amount of information displayed. There was even a selection titled 'More Details' in each section.

"Ah ha!" her mother exclaimed. "Let's try this one." She clicked on 'More Details' and read quickly. "Evelyn Newton. This will do just fine."

"Fine for what, Mom?"

"For a disguise, someone for me to pretend to be, to help the meeting between Alan and Miranda."

"Why that one?"

"Notice this," she replied, pointing at the screen, "Alan and Evelyn dated in college for a few months but haven't seen each other since then, eight years later. That means that Alan will feel comfortable talking to her, but not enough to keep in touch. Since she lives in the Midwest, far from Alan, the chances of them actually meeting are pretty slim. Oh, look, this is perfect! Evelyn has a niece, and it looks like they do lots of stuff together. Now we set the details in our heads and prepare for the part!"

Chapter Eight

Two days later, the whole family was on a plane. Her mother had convinced her father of the separate trips. Julie hadn't heard the conversation, but she figured there'd been talk about mother/daughter bonding time or something like that. The result was they would go to Venture World and the guys to Oceanica Island, meeting up in three days at a wildlife zoo nearby.

    Julie and her mother drove straight from the airport to the hotel and spent the rest of the night reviewing the assignment. In the morning, they confirmed the time when Miranda would be in front of the barrel ride with her twins. Nodding and checking her watch, her mother said, "Let's go! And follow my lead!" As they left the hotel, Julie noticed her mother's hair looked as if she didn't dry it well. She just shrugged it off. The excitement of the assignment was just getting to her, she thought.

They arrived at Venture World right when it opened which left more than two hours before meeting the woman.

"Where do you want to go first?" asked her mother.

"How about all the big rides before the lines get too long?"

"Good idea. We'll beat the crowds."

That's funny, thought Julie. Did Mom put gel in her hair? It looks even darker and maybe a little longer. Probably just a shadow or something.

Even with the assignment looming ahead, Julie was completely enjoying the park. While in line at the second ride, she noticed her mother's hair was definitely longer and… was it a little curly? Her nose also looked odd.

Of course! Julie felt like kicking herself and just barely held her hand back from smacking her forehead. She was changing to her new disguise! But why so slowly? Why not before they left the hotel? She fought down her questions and paid closer attention to the details.

About an hour later, her mother was altered even more. Her nose was longer and Julie would swear she was a little taller. Next, there was the hint of a cleft in her chin and soon the only thing she could recognize were her mother's green eyes. If she hadn't been there the whole time, Julie wouldn't have known this was her mother. It was still a bit spooky, but Julie was getting used to the prickles and shivers.

Out of curiosity, she studied her own reflection in a

window while standing in line. Nope. Same old Julie, straight-as-straw light brown hair, thick eyebrows and medium complexion with a few scattered freckles. Well, she didn't think she would change but it would have been nice to see something different!

"How about this one next?" asked her mother. Julie looked up, startled. They had managed to end up in front of the barrel ride at, (she glanced at her watch), yes, near the correct time. She looked at her mother, whose eyes were now brown and twinkling at her.

"Just do what seems natural," she whispered.

As they approached the line, a little boy of about two suddenly ran toward them. Julie automatically knelt and held out her arms to block his flight.

"Whoa, little guy. Where are you going? Where's your mommy or daddy?" The little boy giggled. Julie looked around and spied a young woman struggling with a stroller and holding the hand of an identical toddler trying to follow his brother. With a start, Julie recognized the woman as the client, Miranda Alvarez.

Wow, Mom *was* good.

"Let's get this little one back to his mother, shall we?" Julie jerked involuntarily. Her mother's voice had changed, a little higher and just a bit nasally.

"Oh, thank you so much," said the young woman breathlessly as they approached. Half her hair had come loose from the barrettes and her face was flushed. Her eyes were red with a suggestion of tears. "What ever made me think I could handle this?"

"You know, Holly is great with kids." *Holly*? Oh, yeah, the niece. "Why don't we wait behind you and she can entertain them." Her mom gave Julie a barely noticeable wink then thrust her hand toward Miranda. "My name is Evelyn Newton."

The woman introduced herself and her twins warily, but also with a bit of relief. As they stood in line, Julie kept the twins amused and listened to her mom and Miranda talk.

"My husband died a little over a year ago. All my friends thought this outing would be good for us," Miranda was saying as she used her free hand to sweep her hair out of her eyes. "You notice none of them came with me!"

As they talked, Julie realized that everything her mother said matched the information they had gathered. Her mother was careful to mention which college she went to (same as the other client) and spoke of "Holly" as a niece, not a daughter.

After the ride, they stayed with Miranda and the twins. When their client tried to demur again, saying that surely Holly and Evelyn had other things to do, 'Evelyn' waved away her protests and said it was no problem.

"Besides," added Julie-Holly, "We've already been to all the big rides and wanted to go on these anyway!" It seemed to be the right thing to say since, after that, Miranda seemed to relax and have fun. When the twins started yawning between rides, Miranda had to call it a day. Julie hadn't even noticed it was almost dinnertime!

"Are you coming here tomorrow, too?" her mother asked. When Miranda nodded, Annette-Evelyn suggested they meet again. Miranda seemed a little unsure, as if she really would like to but didn't want to impose.

Julie decided it was time for her to make another contribution.

"Oh, that would be wonderful! Seeing all the kid's rides is so much more fun with Jason and Jeremy!"

Apparently that did the trick. The young mother agreed to meet them in the morning and then have lunch together. Back at the hotel, her mother beamed at Julie and nearly crushed her in a hug. "I am so proud of you! You're a natural, just like I thought you would be! Let's have some dinner!"

The next morning, Julie was momentarily shocked to see a dark-haired stranger until it penetrated her sleep-fogged mind that her mother was still in disguise. She had been "Evelyn" all through dinner and obviously never changed back. Now that they were alone, she asked her mother about yesterday's slow change.

"Well," her mother replied. "I figured it would be a bit

easier for you to adjust to Evelyn gradually. You know, get used to the new me!"

Julie smiled. "I didn't even realize you were doing it for over an hour. Even when I started watching for changes, I didn't see anything actually happen. But why haven't you changed back?"

"It takes quite a bit of energy and concentration to change back so I just stayed Evelyn. Now, we have to eat breakfast so we can meet Miranda on time!"

After they met Miranda and the twins, the day went pretty much the same as the day before. Julie had a great time at the park, nearly forgetting the reason they were there. The entire group had just sat down for lunch in a crowded outdoor café when her mother stood back up and called, "Alan? Alan Hoskin?"

A man was walking by, a large food tray in his right hand and a little girl holding the left. He had clearly been looking for a place to sit.

"It's me, Evelyn, from college." When Alan hesitated, her mother added, "Professor Schmidt's English class, if I remember correctly."

"Why yes! Evie! Of course! How are you doing?"

"Just fine! Why don't you sit with us and we'll catch up."

"Since I can't seem to find an open table, I'll take you up on that!" Alan said with a grin.

When they were settled, introductions were made. Alan introduced his five-year-old daughter, Alicia, who kept her eyes glued to her plate, occasionally sneaking glances at everyone.

They chatted for a while about old school buddies. Now Julie understood why her mother had spent all that time researching Alan.

"Are you on vacation, Alan, or do you live near here?" asked Annette-Evie.

"Actually, it's sort of a working vacation. I've been offered a job so I've been checking out the area all week. I decided to stay the extra weekend to spend time with Alicia. She's the main reason I want to come back." He smiled down at his daughter.

"What a coincidence! Miranda lives nearby." She grinned impishly. "Maybe she can help you find your way around."

"I'd be happy to," said Miranda with a glowing blush and a smile just for Alan.

The job was done.

Chapter Nine

"Wow, that was great!" Julie said, back in their room. "Only a day and a half and you changed their lives! Did you see the way the twins acted with Alicia? They totally forgot about me and made her their new playmate! She even stopped being shy and took charge of the twins. Will Miranda and Alan get married? Is that all we need to do? What's next?"

"Whoa!" Her mother, no longer "Evelyn", held up her hands and laughed. "I guess I don't need to ask you if you'd like to continue!"

"You bet! When can I start?"

"First, we should talk a little more about the job and all that comes with it."

Julie grabbed two cans of root beer out of the little refrigerator and put them on the table within easy reach. Her mother sat directly in front of her.

"Number one," her mother began. "I've said it before but it bears repeating; you must keep this a secret. You can't talk about it to anyone."

"Not even Carrie?"

"Not even your best friend." Her mother sighed. "I know from experience it's difficult and sometimes very lonely. Your father knows about QPID but I hardly ever discuss my assignments with him. I can't tell you how glad I am that I can finally talk to you about it." She squeezed Julie's knee. "Anyway, continuing on, rule number two. You must never abuse your privileges and power of the position you have." She put a finger under Julie's chin, tipped her head up and looked her straight in the eyes. "This is very serious. You are given lots of information and Benefits and they must be used appropriately or suffer the consequences."

"Why? What would happen?"

"You'd lose all Benefits and, as I mentioned earlier, you'd be banned from QPID. You also would remember nothing about the program at all." Julie nodded.

"You must do your assignment as it is given to you, although you can refuse if you want. For the first few assignments, you'll be supervised closely and required to make regular reports. You'll be an apprentice until you pass your first several assignments successfully and are accepted as a full-time member."

"Who'll supervise me?" Julie asked.

"I will, if you want, but if you'd rather have someone else, I understand."

"No way, Mom," she replied, rather vehemently. "I can't think of anyone I'd rather have!" She jumped up and gave her mother a quick hug. When she sat down again, she could have sworn she saw tears in her mother's eyes.

Her mother cleared her throat, blinking rapidly. "So those are the most important rules. We'll discuss other things as they come up. Any questions?"

Julie thought for a minute, trying to pick a question out of the dozens that were zooming around her brain.

"What are some other Benefits or privileges?"

"There are lots of them and no one has them all, only those that help you with your jobs. You know about changing your appearance, and there is also knowledge, which comes in many different forms. The first kind you have is the information you get with the assignments. Another is a kind of knowledge of what to say or do in certain situations. One common Benefit is the Temporary Talent. You can probably guess what that is."

"Probably temporarily having a talent like car racing if you need to meet an Indy 500 driver!" she joked.

"Exactly!" her mother replied, to Julie's surprise. "Now," she continued. "Shall we sign you up?"

Her mother set the laptop on the table between them and booted up. As soon as she logged on to QPID, a message popped up.

"Welcome, Julie Hatcher. Please select your identification and password so we can create your file."

Julie's mouth dropped open yet again. She just couldn't get used to this magic stuff! She looked at her mother, expecting the usual knowing smile, but her mother's jaw had actually dropped, too. Before Julie could comment, her mother blinked several times and turned to grin at her.

"Well, that was easy! So, what do you want for a code name? It should be something simple. Easy to remember but not obvious."

As they discussed a codename, Julie eyed her mother. Had her mother truly been surprised at the welcome message? She had recovered so quickly, Julie now thought maybe it was just her imagination. And how did QPID know she was willing to sign on? Her curiosity about QPID multiplied. The only thing that kept her from grilling her mother was the warning about not asking too many questions.

"So, any ideas, Jule?"

"That's it!"

"What's it?"

"Jule, only spelled J-E-W-E-L." Julie was pretty proud of this solution.

"Good, but you need a number, too."

"Ok, two. 'Jewel2' I like it."

"So do I," said her mother and she typed it in. "Now, when you first log on at home, they will ask you for a password so be ready for that." She hit the Enter key with a flourish. "All done."

"When do I get my first assignment?" Her fingers itched to begin typing.

"Probably not until we get home."

Julie's shoulders slumped and she couldn't suppress a groan. Her mother closed the laptop and chuckled.

"Give it time!" she said. "Your file has to be set up and then an assignment decided on. It could take a week or even a couple of months. You never really know exactly when you'll get an assignment."

"Why not?"

"There might not be any jobs in the area, like what happened with our first request, or someone else might be better suited to do it."

"Someone else? Just how many QPID members are there?"

Her mother simply blinked. "I have no idea. I've never really thought about it."

"Well," said Julie, determined not to let it go, "How many have you met?"

Her mother shifted uncomfortably in her chair. "The only one I have ever met is your Grandma, and that's because she was my mentor."

"That's right; you said it was a family business. How far back does it go?"

"I know my mother, grandmother and great-grandmother all worked for QPID, but before that, I don't know. Nobody ever told me."

When Julie drew breath for another question, her mother held up her hand. "I can't tell you very many details. I told you that certain questions would *not* be answered. I was a little curious too, but never found out much." Her mother's face became expressionless. "Don't ask any more of those questions."

"All right." She didn't want to upset her mother, but not knowing just made it more intriguing. Why the extreme secrecy? Someday she would find out, she promised herself. For now, she changed the subject.

"Have you had any really great assignments?"

"A few."

"What's your favorite?"

Her mother smiled and became relaxed and animated again. "That's easy." She sat back, hands on her crossed knees. "In college, I managed to get two people to meet without ever talking to either one of them!"

"Really?" exclaimed Julie. "How?"

Her mother stared into the distance. "Well, for starters they were both athletic but he played racquetball and she took fencing. She was a freshman and he was a senior so I had a difficult time finding common ground. However," her mother's eyes gleamed, "for the spring semester I did some fiddling with the classes and registration. I made sure there was no advanced fencing class so the girl would have to choose something else. As it happened, the racquetball class was closed so she signed up for tennis instead. I had signed up in the same racquetball class in order to get them to meet, but she wouldn't get in if I didn't take drastic measures. Luckily," she winked, "the computer lost her pre-registration information. Then she had to register by hand. Back then, that meant you had to elbow your way through a crowded auditorium to gather class cards for the classes you wanted. I saw to it," her mother winked again, "that tennis was full. Just as she was almost finished, I canceled my racquetball class so there was an opening. At first I thought she would just walk by and never notice it. But I brushed up against her, making her almost lose her stack of class cards. She stopped to straighten them, looked up, saw the opening for racquetball and signed up." Her mother grinned with the memory. "They ended up being racquetball partners and then started dating. I had never spoken to either one."

"Wow." Julie was impressed. "Tell me more!"

"Okay, once there were these two men who both liked the same woman...."

They talked late into the night about the job and her mother's experiences. When they finally went to bed, Julie was more excited than ever about joining this magical, mysterious thing called QPID.

Chapter Ten

During the rest of the trip Julie longed to talk more with her mother. However, early the next day they met her father and Stuart at the zoo, so they didn't get the chance to be alone. It was late Wednesday night when their plane landed, so the whole family had a quick dinner then went straight to bed.

Julie was too keyed up to sleep. She grabbed one of her favorite books and read for an hour before she felt sleepy. Finally, she set the book on the nightstand and turned out the lamp.

It seemed like she had just fallen asleep when she came suddenly awake. It must have been a noise, she decided. She could hear nothing now though she strained her ears. She turned over to check the time and caught her breath. There was something lying on top of her book on the nightstand, reflected in the light of the digital clock.

Slowly she sat up and switched on her reading lamp. It was an envelope made of a shimmering paper with changing rainbows of colors. It couldn't have been there when she went to sleep. Julie was suddenly reminded of the time she "caught" the tooth fairy. She'd always been a light sleeper. The sound of the door closing must have been what awakened her. She relaxed and grinned as she reached for the envelope.

Inside was a beautiful card with the same rainbow colors. She opened the card and written in graceful, metallic letters, was a simple message:

"Welcome to the organization, Julie Hatcher. Great things are expected. Good luck. QPID"

A nice card, but what did it mean? Great things? Expected of the organization or of her? She would have to remember to ask her mother in the morning. Laying the card and envelope atop her book on the nightstand, she switched off the lamp.

As soon as the sun hit her bedroom window, Julie leapt out of bed, grabbed the nearest clothes and dressed as she raced downstairs. Despite nearly tripping twice as she put on her shorts, she was at the computer logging in before the rest of her family woke up. She typed in her own name and code and waited, fingers drumming on the mouse pad. Her pulse raced as a message scrolled across: "Welcome, Jewel2!" She felt a thrill, seeing her very own codename on the screen. "Create your password, please." Julie had thought hard about this and typed in "Fudgie." That was the name of the brown cat that the family had had since she was two. He had died last year and she still missed him.

The computer beeped acceptance of the password. "Your assignment will be posted in four days." It was official! She was a member!

Elated, she logged off and shut the computer down, then headed into the kitchen for some cereal. Who would it be? Girls? Boys? Or both? Will it be someone she knows? Her mother had said the first assignments are usually friends, fairly simple to begin with. Would she get any Benefits? Four days started to seem like a long time!

The phone rang, interrupting her train of thought. A little annoyed, Julie answered. "Hello."

"So? How was Oceanica Island?" It was Carrie.

"Huh?"

"The trip, dummy!"

Julie had forgotten that she hadn't had a chance to tell Carrie about the change in plans. Caught off guard, she had to think fast. "Actually, Mom and I went to Venture World instead."

"What? Why?"

"Mom wanted to have a trip with just me and her. Um,

I guess it was just a mother/daughter thing, you know, now that we are going to junior high, you know." Did that sound convincing enough? Luckily, Carrie was easily distracted.

"Yeah, a whole new school! Only four days away, can you believe it?" Carrie asked. "What do you think the teachers will be like?"

School! Even though she'd been anticipating it all summer, junior high school had totally slipped from her mind.

"Jule? You there? Hello?"

"Sorry, Carrie, what did you say?"

They talked about school a little longer, her mind only half on the conversation. She hung up and wished she could tell Carrie what the trip had really been about.

"Who was that?"

Julie had been so involved in her thoughts that she hadn't heard her mother come into the kitchen.

"It was Carrie." Her mother gave her a *look* so she added, "We were just talking about junior high." Her mother nodded and went to make her morning tea.

"By the way, Mom, thanks for the card."

"What card?" she asked, filling up the teakettle.

"The card welcoming me to you-know-what." said Julie. Her mother turned the stove on and gave her a peculiar look before answering.

"I didn't give you any card." She cocked her head. "Are

you sure you weren't dreaming?"

"No, of course not. I'll show it to you." She dashed upstairs, straight to the nightstand by her bed. Her hand froze mid-reach as she realized the card was no longer on her book. She was sure she'd left it there! She looked all around her room and even under the bed. No card. What happened to it? Julie sat on the bed. Surely it couldn't have been a dream! She could picture the card so clearly! It had to be real.

Somewhat embarrassed, she decided not to bring up the subject again to her mother unless she found it or her mother asked about it. To her surprise, her mother never asked.

Chapter Eleven

Julie woke up full of energy. It was hard to tell which she was more excited about, junior high or her first QPID assignment. She got up early to log on to QPID, but nothing new was posted. She told herself to put QPID out of her mind and focus on school. On the bus, she compared her schedule again with Carrie.

"We have the first two classes together," Carrie said, "and then science classes only two doors away. English is again together, and then we go to lunch."

"I hope finding our classrooms won't be too hard," said Julie.

"After lunch you're on your own, Jule," said Carrie good-naturedly. "It's not my fault that you wanted to take Computers instead of Art."

Julie almost commented that it was a good thing,

seeing as how she was going to be using the computer a lot, but stopped herself just in time. She'd nearly blown the secret! She'd better be more careful!

"What did you learn from your sister about the teachers?" she asked Carrie.

"Well, you know that Elaine had Mrs. Moon for English two years ago and said she was a pretty good teacher. Lots of reading and homework, but not too hard. She didn't know about either of our science teachers, but she did warn me about Mr. Vallance in History."

Julie's eyes widened and the girls put their heads together. Carrie lowered her voice.

"Elaine said that he always picks on one or two students each semester. As long as we don't do anything to stand out, he probably won't notice us and we'll be okay."

"Good to know!"

Carrie plopped her lunch tray next to Julie. "Isn't this great?" she asked. "We can pick whatever we want for lunch now, no menus." Julie nodded, her mouth full of ham and cheese. "Ah! Pizza every day," said Carrie and she took a huge bite, cheese stringing down her chin.

Julie swallowed quickly. "Over here Brenna, Sarah," she hollered, waving.

"Wow, that's a huge cheeseburger, Brenna,"

observed Carrie.

"Gotta make it through my soccer game after school." She crooked a thumb at Sarah who was rolling her eyes. "Her puny salad wouldn't last me an hour!"

"Vegetarians don't eat cheeseburgers," replied Sarah loftily.

"I keep telling you, Sarah," Brenna said as she squirted mustard and ketchup on her burger. "You'd have done a lot better at soccer with a few cheeseburgers in you!"

"I was only five! Here!" Sarah tossed a couple of cucumber slices on Brenna's plate. "Maybe some veggies will help you in Music."

As Brenna shuddered away from the cucumbers, Julie and Carrie grinned at each other. The two girls' antics were legendary. They seemed like enemies but had been the best of friends since that first soccer team. Even when Sarah's parents gave in to the inevitable and decided Sarah's talents were not in sports but music, they remained inseparable.

"So," said Brenna, turning to Julie and Carrie. "I hear that you guys had Mr. Vallance, the pirate, for first hour."

Sarah gasped. "How'd it go?"

"We just kept our mouths shut and avoided eye contact," replied Carrie. "No problem, although you're right. That messy hair and nasty scowl do make him look like a pirate. All he needs is an eye patch!" Carrie and Brenna giggled while Sarah looked on disapprovingly. Julie decided she had better change the subject.

"I'm glad we're all together in Math second hour."

"I like Ms. Mahoney," said Sarah. "She's so bubbly, I think Math will actually be fun."

"Speak for yourself," said Julie. "You know I'm going to need all the help I can get."

"As long as you help me read all those books for English," replied Carrie. "I don't know where I'll find the time! Mrs. Moon must think all we have to do in life is read."

Julie shrugged. "I've already read some of them."

"Of course you have, bookworm," commented Brenna, now digging into her fries.

Sarah glared at Brenna again. "What's Biology like, Julie?"

Julie groaned. "After energetic Ms. Mahony, I nearly fell asleep. All Mrs. Dobbins did was sit on her stool droning on about flowers. It looks like we'll be studying flowers for about six weeks from what was on the syllabus."

It was Brenna's turn to groan. "Raise your hand if you are sick of all those syllabuses!" Four hands shot up simultaneously with even a few from those seated nearby. The whole group laughed.

As the conversation turned toward afternoon classes, Julie looked around the lunchroom. She noticed that there were quite a few students sitting all by themselves. Everybody's shy on the first day, she thought. But this is even worse because it's junior high with kids from other schools and different classes. She looked back at her three friends. Brenna was leaning across the table to give advice for the afternoon gym class. Julie was glad they were here.

"I wish I had taken gym as my last class like you," said Carrie on the bus ride home. "Everybody has to shower except for the last class of the day." Carrie nudged Julie with her elbow. "Just don't get too close in those sweaty gym clothes."

"Don't worry. I'll be starting swimming soon and I'll ride the bus with you only a couple days a week."

"Here's my stop. See you tomorrow," said Carrie.

As the bus approached her house, Julie suddenly recalled her QPID assignment. She hoped that it would be posted by now. The day had been busy enough that she had had no more temptations to talk about it.

Now was different. She got off the bus and raced in the front door. With an expert toss, her backpack landed squarely in the nearest corner and Julie headed for the computer. She skidded to a halt when she saw her little brother already on it, playing a long game. What now?

"When are you getting off?" she asked her brother.

"I just got on! Why?"

"I've got to…" she paused, gritting her teeth. Just then her mother, already home from work, walked in. Julie changed her sentence quickly. "I've got an assignment." Her hands clenching and unclenching, she looked at her mother.

"On the first day of school?" Stuart replied. "Boy, I'm sure glad I'm not in junior high!"

"Already?" Her mother gave Julie a sharp look. "You can use my computer if you're not too long. Let me help you log on."

She gave her mother a big smile and followed her upstairs, close on her heels. When the door was closed, she said "Thanks Mom!"

"Just be careful what you say, even to Stuart or Dad."

"But you said that Dad knows."

"Well, yes, he does know about QPID but we usually don't discuss it at all. And I haven't told him about you yet."

"Why not?" she asked.

Her mother was quiet for a while before answering. "It's hard to explain. First, I figured I don't need to tell him until you have definitely decided to be a permanent member. Second, about me as an agent, I had to tell him so he could understand some of the things I need to do, but I don't know if he truly believes about most of it." She sighed. "I suppose that he thinks of it as a hobby of mine and doesn't take it seriously. I tried talking to him once or twice but he's never shown any interest in QPID at all. So, until now I've only talked about it with your grandma. But she lives in Oregon and we don't see each other that often."

"Grandma? Does she still work for QPID?" Julie asked, incredulous.

"Of course," her mother replied. "Just because you get older doesn't mean you quit meeting people."

"Yeah, I guess," she mumbled, a little embarrassed, but an idea occurred to her. Maybe Grandma would know more details about QPID. She started to make a mental list of things to ask her next time she had the chance, but her mother's next words interrupted her flow of thought.

"Let's see what your new job is!"

Julie logged on. There was her first assignment! She was to introduce two girls that happened to be her age. She knew one, a girl at her school named Tammy Heron, but the other girl she had never heard of. Susan Fox attended another school nearby, but did very few activities. Tammy took dance classes, cheerleading and volleyball. She was very popular with most kids at her school. Julie wondered how to get the two together since there did not seem to be any common interests. And why? They didn't seem to be a match for friends.

"Hmmm," her mother said, reading over Julie's shoulder. "Not a very easy one for beginners, is it? Do you want a suggestion?" Julie nodded. "Meet Susan first and see if a solution comes up." She left to make dinner, telling her to holler if she needed anything else.

Delving further into the details, Julie found out that Susan would be at a nearby park on Thursday evening, watching her brother play soccer. She figured that the park would be a great place to 'run into' Susan. In the picture she had long, blond hair and blue eyes, and looked to be average in height and weight.

This will be easy, Julie thought.

Chapter Twelve

The next three days of school seemed to drag on, but Thursday finally came. Julie rushed through her homework and told her mother she was walking to the park. Her mother looked startled and asked why.

"Just meeting some *friends!*" Julie smiled, suppressing the urge to wink. Her mother grinned back and said, "Okay, but be back before dark."

"No problem, Mom," and she was out the door.

It was a beautiful afternoon and she enjoyed the mile walk. She could hear the sounds of kids playing before turning the final corner. Suddenly her heart began to pound and her mouth went dry. It was just like the time she had to give a speech to the entire fifth grade.

Julie slowed down as she wiped her damp palms on her shorts. She had never considered herself to be very outgoing and had never really tried hard to make new friends. How do people meet, anyway? She thought back to how she met Carrie. Julie and her family had only been in the new house for two weeks. By the third day of second grade, all the old friends from first grade had paired off. She had been reading *Black Beauty* during lunch when Carrie came up and asked if she liked horses. Carrie then launched into tales all about how she'd been riding since she was four. From that day on they were buddies. Carrie was already friends with Brenna from growing up on the same street. Brenna, of course, knew Sarah from the soccer team.

    None of this really helped Julie now with the QPID assignment. Especially since she wasn't sure if she could be like Carrie and just go up to Susan and start talking. What if Susan didn't want to talk to her? What if she was mean or even just shy? Perhaps this wouldn't be as easy as she thought. Well, no use worrying about what Susan was like until she met her! Getting up the nerve to strike up a conversation with someone she didn't know would be hard enough. Julie firmly told the butterflies in her stomach to settle down. She picked up her pace and continued to the park.

    As she arrived, she noticed her first problem. There were four different soccer games going on and a lot more people than she thought there would be. She approached the fields and saw the first game was all girls. Since she knew Susan was watching her brother, she kept walking. The other three teams were all boys and there were a lot of people watching. Julie made a slow circuit of the fields, trying to act casual.

After one trip around the park, Julie was rather desperate. There were three girls about the right size with long blond hair and similar features. She wished she had studied Susan's picture more, but she had no idea it would be this difficult. One girl with tight braids was close by, screaming as loudly as she could for a team in green shirts. The second girl was sitting on a blanket with two other girls, watching a game between red uniforms and blue ones. The third was on the far side, sitting quietly on a bench, alternating reading and clapping for the team playing against the green shirts.

What should she do? She couldn't just go up and ask each girl if her name was Susan, could she? No, it would be too conspicuous.

"Should've studied more," she muttered to herself. The near girl seemed to be yelling for a guy named Brad. Julie edged a little closer. Was that the name of Susan's brother? She couldn't remember! The blond also seemed to know a lot about the game.

Suddenly, she had an inspiration! She moved slowly along the sidelines, pretending to be engrossed in the game. She was right next to the blond when the referee blew his whistle. The girl seemed disgusted with the call, shaking her head, braids whipping dangerously back and forth.

"What happened?" she asked the girl. "I didn't see it."

The girl turned to her and said, "The ref called a foul on Jim."

"Foul?" Julie asked. When the girl gave her a strange look, she added, "I don't know much about soccer."

"Oh," she shrugged and pointed at the field, "the referee claimed that Jim intentionally tripped a player on the other team. But he just was trying to get the ball. Come on Crocodiles! Score!"

"You seem to know a lot about it. Do you play soccer?" Julie asked.

"Sure. Any sport I can!" she replied, eyes glued on the game. Julie smiled to herself, sure this wasn't her client. She distinctly remembered that Susan did very few activities and no sports.

"Thanks!" she said to the blond, who waved absently over her shoulder while again yelling at the players.

Julie made her way to the group of girls on the blanket. It took several minutes of eavesdropping to determine that the blond was named Natalie. The good news was, she'd found Susan. The bad news was, the games were over and the sun was going down. She looked over to the bench where Susan had been sitting, all the way across the park. Susan was already walking away with what must be her brother and mother.

It was all Julie could do to keep from crying out to Susan as she disappeared from sight. She'd failed! Failed to meet her first client and now she couldn't introduce her to Tammy. She started to walk home, eyes on her dragging feet. She kicked stray pebbles, angry with herself for blowing her first assignment. Caught up in her misery, Julie paid no attention to where she went.

Suddenly her head came up as she felt a silent warning. It was almost dark and she didn't know where she was! Fear shot through her as she looked wildly around.

Calm down, she told herself. She knew these neighborhoods.

She finally recognized the area and realized that she had merely turned down one street too soon. She wasn't lost; she just needed to retrace her steps a block. She tried to convince herself everything was fine, but the uneasy feelings wouldn't go away.

As she started back, Julie caught sight of a beat-up, white car turning onto the street, going very slowly. She froze and stared at it. Her gut tensed and her body went cold all over. She was suddenly sure, she *knew,* that the car, or who was in it, was dangerous. The instinct was so strong, she was positive she shouldn't walk past it. Her way home was cut off!

What now? She began to walk fast, away from the car, going further down the street. The car was still far enough away that the driver probably hadn't seen her in the twilight. Her heart began to pound and she couldn't get rid of the feeling of *knowing* she was in danger. As the car's headlights popped on, she broke into a run. The street curved a little so she figured she was still out of sight of whoever was in the car. A quick glance over her shoulder caused her to trip and fall right in front of a house with huge bushes near the sidewalk. She scrambled on her hands and knees to hide behind the bushes.

Her breathing was ragged. The whole neighborhood must be able to hear her beating heart. Where was everybody? In their houses, eating dinner, she thought wryly, wishing that she was doing the same. She held her breath as the car crept closer. She peered through the bushes but all she could see was the headlights. They shone on the bushes for just a moment and she flattened herself on the ground. Fear ran through her again.

The car continued past and Julie released her breath explosively. She didn't move, however, until it was completely out of sight. As the car rounded another corner, she stood up, ears straining for any hint of it returning. Finally, she stepped back onto the sidewalk and realized that it was almost full night. She was very late. She ran most of the way home, but stopped on the front porch to catch her breath.

Taking slow, deep breaths, Julie thought about what had happened and started feeling a little silly. She didn't know who was in the car and really had no reason to think that there was any danger. She hadn't been thinking straight, focused instead on her botched assignment. She laughed at herself. Why, that car might have been just looking for a particular address or a lost dog or something.

Smells of dinner wafted to her as she opened the front door. Oh, no, she was going to be in trouble. Her shoulders slumped as she closed the front door. She glanced at the hall tree mirror and gasped as she saw her hair was full of twigs. And her knee, she realized, was scraped from the fall. She dashed toward the bathroom as her mother called from the kitchen.

"Is that you, Julie? Why are you late?"

"I just lost track of time, Mom." She hastily washed her hands and tidied herself up as best she could.

"Well, hurry, dinner is already on the table," her mother replied. Julie grimaced at her reflection. Her mother did not sound happy.

"Where have you been?" asked her father sternly. "I was just getting ready to come looking for you."

Julie sat down and forced a smile.

"One of the soccer games went late and I didn't realize how dark it was getting with the lights at the park and all." She scooped up some peas and plopped them next to her chicken on the plate. She looked only at her food, quite aware of her parents' disapproval.

"That's not like you," her mother commented. "Is something wrong?"

"No, just didn't pay attention." She glanced at her mother and shook her head slightly. She kept thinking, "Please don't ask, please," as if her mother could read her thoughts. Her mother's eyes narrowed as she said, "We'll discuss this later."

The tense mood slowly evaporated as dinner passed. Julie tried to act as if nothing had happened, but it didn't help that Stuart kept mouthing silently "You're in trouble!"

After dinner, while she was finishing her homework, her mother came into the room and shut the door.

"All right. Now can you tell me what happened?"

She told her mother what happened with Susan at the park.

"I wasn't paying attention and turned down the wrong street on the way home, so it took longer than I thought." She didn't mention the car at all. She felt embarrassed at her overreaction now that it was all over. She was also a little unsure about how her mother would react to a simple *feeling* that the car was dangerous.

"Just don't let it happen again, okay?" her mother said.

"I won't." But her relief was short-lived.

"No more going to the park by yourself, especially near nighttime. And I'm afraid I'll have to ground you for that lapse in judgment."

"But, Mom...."

"It's not safe for a twelve year old to walk around alone after dark! You could've gotten into serious danger. I'm afraid we both let the excitement of the new job cloud our common sense. No more arguments and grounded for one week."

Julie bit her lip against a retort. Arguing might make the punishment worse. Now she was glad that she hadn't mentioned the car. Her mother would be horrified at what was most likely nothing and she would be grounded for two months!

"Now let's discuss this assignment. You did very well for a beginner."

"I did?"

"Of course. You didn't know there would be that many girls that looked like Susan and you figured out ways to discover the correct one." Her mother smiled. "Not many could improvise that well on the spot. What did you learn?"

"Do more research!" Julie said emphatically. "And I should have studied the picture a little more!"

"Good," her mother patted her knee as she rose to leave. "Let me know what you plan to do next."

"Next?" Julie asked.

"Of course! Your job is not done yet." She chuckled. "You do get more than one try, you know!" Julie felt her spirits lift a little. Maybe she hadn't failed after all.

"Thanks, Mom!"

Chapter Thirteen

"Grounded!" Carrie exclaimed on the bus the next morning. "We were going to go shopping this weekend!"

"I'm sorry."

"What happened? You hardly ever get grounded."

Julie hesitated, not sure what to say. "I got home very late from the park last night." Before she knew it, she was telling Carrie about the car. Why not? It had nothing to do with QPID.

Carrie's eyes widened as Julie described her scramble into the bushes.

"I just felt like something was wrong. I can't explain why."

"Don't knock instinct," Carrie said. "You're better off safe than sorry! I think you did the right thing by hiding." Julie felt much better after unburdening to her best friend. She just wished she could tell Carrie the entire story.

It took a full two weeks for Julie to figure out where to

try to meet Susan again. She had been so busy with school and other activities that she had trouble finding time to do QPID research. Twice, she had some free time, but Stuart was on the computer playing his new game. It was frustrating and the problem was on her mind constantly. Carrie often had to hiss at her to pay attention in class. Julie also found her thoughts wandering at other activities as well.

At last, Julie managed to get on the computer with nobody around. She read that Susan was going to the mall on Saturday. According to the information, Susan would be in front of the food court near lunchtime. By now she had memorized Susan's picture and was sure to pick her out of a crowd.

But how would she actually meet her? Strike up a conversation? About what? Julie liked horseback riding, swimming, and lots of stuff. But she couldn't find anything she had in common with Susan. Well, she would go and perhaps a situation would come up like it did with the twins in her mother's assignment. Meanwhile, she would try to get to know Tammy a little better so it wouldn't be a stranger introducing a stranger.

"Going clothes shopping. Who wants to come?" Julie's mother said. She swung her purse to her shoulder.

Julie immediately spoke up. "Me! I need a new bathing suit."

Her father didn't even look up from the newspaper. "Don't need anything."

Stuart groaned. "Not clothes, again. Why don't we ever go shopping for video games?"

Julie struggled not to smile. Her mother had said she would arrange a trip to the mall with just the two of them without arousing suspicion. She would have to remember this ploy in the future.

They shopped together for an hour or so before her mother left to do some errands elsewhere in the mall. They agreed to meet for lunch at about twelve-thirty.

"Real errands this time," her mother commented, winking at Julie. Julie grinned back then took a deep breath to steady her nerves. Wandering towards the food court, Julie looked in windows and even went into a couple of stores. She even glanced at a few price tags, shook her head, sighed hugely and walked on. She was secretly proud of her acting skills. This secret agent stuff was getting easier.

By the time she reached the food court, it was still about five minutes before Susan was supposed to show up. So she flopped down on a seat as if exhausted and looked around. There was a big crowd heading to get some lunch, but Julie felt confident she would recognize Susan. Yet she still had no idea how to actually meet her. She just couldn't go up and talk to a stranger for no reason. She felt she'd done pretty well at the soccer field, but she knew she'd have to get up her courage all over again. She leaned back and closed her eyes.

"Hello," a voice said. Startled, she opened her eyes and sat up. An elderly man stood in front of her. "Are you all right?" he asked.

Julie was instantly on her guard; girls shouldn't talk to strangers, even in crowded malls. But as she thought that, she *knew* this gentleman was harmless. Even so, she was still wary.

"Just a little tired. Waiting for my friend."

"Okay. Have a nice day!" The man walked away.

Julie relaxed, thinking hard. She knew that he hadn't been dangerous, just like she had felt that the car was. How did she know these things? One would think it would be the other way around. A strange man talking to her certainly seemed scarier than a car. Yet she felt certain she was right in both cases. She just *knew*. Hmm.

Lost in thought, she suddenly realized the time had passed when Susan was supposed to come. She grabbed her bags and jumped up, annoyed with herself. Secret agents didn't get distracted. She had taken no more than three steps when she nearly ran into another person.

"Sorry," said Julie. "I wasn't paying attention." The other person glared and walked away, but the near collision had given her an idea.

She glanced around and caught sight of Susan on the other side of the food court, looking at the restaurants. Nimbly dodging people, Julie made her way around in front of Susan then walked back towards her as if also searching for a place to eat. When Susan glanced at another restaurant, Julie sidestepped and ran into Susan. She faked her fall but to her surprise, Susan fell, too.

"Oh! I'm so sorry!" said Julie, feeling terribly guilty. Guess she overdid it. She quickly got up and helped Susan stand. "Are you okay?" Susan just nodded, a closed look on her face. *Oops, hope I didn't scare her*, thought Julie.

"It was my fault, not paying attention." Susan started to walk away but Julie moved in front of her. "Say, you look familiar. Have we met?"

Susan shook her head.

"I'm sure we have," Julie persisted. "I never forget a face. Let me see," she tapped a finger on her chin. Susan was trying to sidle away so Julie spoke quickly.

"I know." Julie snapped her fingers. "I've seen you at the soccer field before. Actually, about two or three weeks ago, my friend was cheering on the Crocodiles and you were for the other side." Julie nodded. "I remember because you looked like her, but she was screaming her head off and you were sitting quietly. Reading, I think."

Susan just looked down at her shoes and shrugged.

Doesn't she talk? Is she stuck up or what? Julie was running out of ideas. "Do you go to Eastern Junior High?"

"Susan? Did you find a place to eat?" A woman came up and put her arm around Susan's shoulder. She looked at Julie and smiled. "Hello. Who is this, Susan?" Susan's mother, probably.

"Hi, I'm Julie. I accidentally bumped into, um, Susan, is it? I recognized her from the soccer field and was just asking if she went to Eastern Junior High."

"Well, not yet," said the woman. "But we are looking for a house near that school."

Aha! That must have something to do with why she needed to introduce Susan to Tammy, Julie thought. Susan had now edged around behind her mother.

"You see, Susan. You've already found a friend at the new school." Her mother spoke in a soft, gentle voice and gave the girl's shoulders a squeeze. Susan's lip twitched in what might have been an attempt at a smile, but mostly she looked scared at the mention of a new school. "I'm sorry," the mother whispered. "She's very shy."

Oh, that made sense. Julie felt sorry for Susan and really wanted to help now, client or not. Susan seemed like a very nice person, but probably didn't make friends easily.

"Let me give you my phone number," said Julie. "In case you have any questions about the area or school or anything." She smiled what she hoped was a friendly, encouraging smile at Susan. "I'll give you a tour!"

Julie wrote her number on a piece of paper and gave it to Susan.

"Thank you," she said so softly Julie barely heard her.

"Goodbye. It was nice meeting you, Susan." Julie tossed a wave.

Susan's hand came halfway up but it couldn't really be called a wave. "'Bye." She bit her lip. "Julie."

"Maybe I'll see you at the soccer field," said Julie.

Susan hurried off with her mother. Julie smiled, rather pleased with her success, and went to look for her own mother.

Lunch tasted fabulous to Julie, and she couldn't stop grinning. In the car on the way home, she reported everything at top speed to her mother.

"Very good, Julie. What's next?"

"I'm not exactly sure." Julie thought for a moment. "I'll probably concentrate on Tammy for a while until I figure out exactly how to get the two to meet."

Julie's great mood lasted until Monday morning on the school bus. She flopped down on the seat next to Carrie.

"Hi," said Julie.

Carrie crossed her arms and looked out the window. Julie was shocked. Carrie had never done anything like that before.

"What's wrong?" she asked, but Carrie said nothing.

"What is it? Are you mad at me?" Carrie nodded, still looking outside. "But, why?"

Carrie turned and gave her a fierce look. "You know."

Julie was perplexed. She couldn't figure out what she had said or done to make Carrie so angry. "I'm really sorry, Carrie, I just don't know what..."

Carrie looked hurt. "You went to the mall on Saturday, and didn't even tell me you were going!"

"Oh." Now Julie understood, but she didn't know what to say. "How did you know I went to the mall?"

"I called and Stuart told me where you were."

"Nobody told me you called," she said. Carrie just shrugged and looked out the window again.

"Look, I'm sorry," said Julie as the silence stretched on and on. "It was a last minute thing with my mom. I don't know why you're so upset about it."

"It's not just that, Jule. You've been acting weird for weeks, staring off into space and pretending like I don't exist anymore. Brenna and Sarah have noticed, too. In fact, it's been going on since school started."

"That's not true!"

"Oh yeah?" snapped Carrie as she whipped her head around again. "I bet you don't even remember me saying last week that I needed some jeans and I wanted to go shopping. Also that I had put it off the weekend before because you were grounded."

Julie was stung. It was true. She vaguely remembered Carrie saying something of the sort but couldn't recall any details. Had she really been that focused on her new job with QPID? "I...I..." she stammered.

"Never mind. If you don't want to be friends anymore, you should just tell me. Instead you ignore me. Two can play at that game." Carrie's voice quavered as she looked away.

They sat in silence the rest of the way to school. Julie felt horrible. She'd been neglecting her own friendship for the sake of someone else's.

When they got to school, Carrie walked straight to class, not looking back. Julie dragged her feet and arrived just as the bell rang.

All through class she brooded. She didn't even care that Mr. Vallance was eyeing her and Carrie strangely. How could I do that to my best friend? She realized that was probably the first time that she had gone to the mall without Carrie since they met. For the hundredth time she wished she could tell Carrie about QPID. It would make things so much easier. Working for a secret agency seemed so cool, it had never occurred to Julie it might not be all fun and games. A hard assignment was bad enough, but now the secrecy was hurting her relationship with Carrie. Maybe she shouldn't even work for QPID if she couldn't even keep her own friendships straight.

Chapter Fourteen

As the days went by, Julie lost more and more hope. Carrie still avoided her and she hadn't heard a word from Susan. She felt like a failure and wondered why she was still bothering to try to work on her QPID assignment. Her mother had said she really didn't have to become an agent. Maybe quitting would solve things with Carrie.

After enduring four days of the silent treatment from Carrie, she was walking to what would probably be another lonely lunch when she passed Tammy in the hall.

"Hi, Julie," she said. "How's it going?"

Julie looked up, surprised. "Fine, thanks," came the automatic answer.

"Great, see you around!" Tammy gave a quick wave and walked on by.

Julie waved after her, spirits lifting. Her efforts to make

friends with Tammy must be going better than she thought. Julie smiled for the first time in days, and she hurried toward the cafeteria. It was time to set things right with Carrie.

All week she'd been thinking what to say to Carrie. Julie would apologize, of course, but she also wanted to explain why things had been so strange lately. She knew she couldn't tell Carrie the real reasons but she didn't want to lie either. Until this moment, she couldn't seem to get past this dilemma. She glanced around the cafeteria and spotted Carrie eating lunch alone. Julie knew exactly what to say.

"Carrie, I need to talk to you." Carrie just shrugged and said okay, pushing fruit around on her lunch plate with a fork. That was the most she'd said to Julie all week. Encouraged, Julie sat down next to her friend.

"First of all, I'm sorry for everything that's been happening. It's my fault and I would like to explain what it's all about." Carrie looked at her, clearly willing to listen. Julie took a deep breath and continued. "It started with the trip I went on with Mom, to Venture World. It wasn't anything huge, just mother/daughter time like I said. But we talked a lot and she brought up something that has had me distracted for a while."

"What?" said Carrie as she put down her fork.

"She asked about the future, and what I might want to do as a career when I grow up. I've been thinking hard about that because I don't have any idea what I'd like to be."

"Why didn't you just tell me?"

"I don't know, Carrie. I guess because ever since I've known you, you've known that you want to be either a tennis player or horse trainer. I've never even thought about it until Mom asked and now," Julie sighed, "I still have no idea. It's been really bugging me and I didn't notice that I was ignoring you until you got mad. And…well, I'm really sorry."

"Oh, that's okay. I forgive you." Carrie said. Julie felt weak with relief. Carrie stuck her nose up in the air and said jokingly, "Although I'm not sure you deserve it. Don't you know you can tell me anything?"

Julie laughed, heart feeling lighter. "Well, terribly sorry, O Wise One. I'll never doubt you again!" The girls collapsed into giggles. "Oh, Carrie. What would I do without you?"

"You'd probably still be reading by yourself at lunch and definitely not riding horses!" The reminder of Julie's first lonely week in second grade caused an image of Susan to pop in her head. A new school would be twice as hard for crushingly shy Susan. Suddenly, Julie knew what she had to do. What QPID had to help her do. However she and QPID could help Susan, she would!

"So let me help you figure out what you want to be when you grow up!" Carrie pursed her lips. "I hope it has nothing to do with math! Ooh, how about a horse trainer like me? You could be my assistant! Maybe a vet so I could get cheap horse care! Ooh, what about…"

Julie was happier than she'd been all week. She didn't give away any secrets and told just the right amount of truth. Not really lying since, after all, her mother did ask if she wanted to have QPID as a career! And now, she was more determined than ever to be the best agent possible!

Chapter Fifteen

Deciding to be the best agent and actually doing so were two entirely different things as Julie discovered. More time slipped away without hearing from Susan. After two weeks, she decided to try the soccer field again to see if she could find Susan.

When that didn't work, she reconsidered how to get the two girls together. Mad at herself for not getting Susan's phone number, she figured she would have to start from the beginning. But after three constant days of research, she was still at a loss and needed some advice.

"Mom? Can I ask you something?" Her mother put down her pen and pushed her work to the side as she motioned Julie into the room. Julie sat on the bed and told her what had happened, or hadn't happened, so far with Susan and Tammy.

"I have no idea what to do next," she said. "Both girls

do totally different things. Tammy is in dance, cheerleading, gymnastics and lots of other clubs while Susan is only in the chess club and the Honor Society. I can't find anything in common between them." Julie stood up and started pacing, arms crossing and uncrossing. "They even act differently. Tammy is very popular with lots of friends and Susan is very shy, almost ... invisible. She has trouble just talking to people." She stopped and looked at her mother who merely nodded. "In fact, I don't even think they can be friends, no matter what I do." She took a deep breath. "I know Susan needs a friend but why Tammy? Why not match her up with someone else more like her?"

Her mother didn't say a word but sat with hands folded, looking thoughtful. Julie started pacing again and just as the silence began to grow uncomfortable, her mother spoke softly.

"There's no doubt that this is a difficult first assignment. It's very unusual. All I had to do on my first job was introduce two people that I already knew! I'm not sure why you have been started on one that is so challenging. It seems great things are expected from you. " Julie stopped in her tracks and stared at her mother. Where had she heard that before? Oh yeah, that mysterious card. Yet her mother had said she knew nothing about that! Even now she seemed oblivious to Julie's reaction and continued talking.

"It's quite natural to question your assignments at first,

especially when they are tough. But don't you see that you are needed? These girls would never meet on their own, yet for some reason, it's very necessary that they do."

Julie sank to the bed, beginning to understand. But why would QPID pick those two? Her mother's next words echoed Julie's thoughts. "I don't know why they have to be introduced and it's likely that you won't ever know either. There is a bit of trust needed between you and QPID. They trust that you do your job and you trust that they know what they are doing. Friendship may not even be needed, just an introduction. Understand?"

Julie smacked her forehead. "Why didn't I think of that? It's so obvious now. You even mentioned something like that before."

"You're new at this. Don't get distracted by wanting to know 'why.' Just focus on getting the two to meet. Now," she opened her laptop. "Let's see if we can't solve this!"

As the computer was booting up, she gave Julie a thoughtful look.

"What?" said Julie.

"I'm just thinking that since they gave you a difficult assignment, they might be willing to give you something extra."

"Like what?"

"One of the Benefits that can help you in a job." Her mother shook her head. "They usually don't give any extras this early, but they might make an exception in your case. Ah, it's ready. Go ahead, log on."

As Julie typed in her username and password, she wondered if this would be one of the privileges that her mother had mentioned before, like shape changing. Her mother waved her hand at the computer. "Do you notice anything different?"

She peered at the screen. "There's an option that wasn't there before. It says 'Need to know' and has a place for me to type something! But... but..." She shook her head and rubbed the back of her neck.

"What's wrong?" her mother asked, a smile tugging at the corners of her mouth.

"How did they know?" Yet again, QPID knew exactly what was going on and what was needed. Her mother did not seem as surprised this time but did look at Julie a little oddly.

"They just know. Now, what do you want to ask?" Julie had to force her thoughts back to the immediate problem.

"Um, I'd like to know if, or I mean when, Susan is coming to our neighborhood and school."

"All right, type it in."

Julie entered the question and sat back. A tiny man wearing a tuxedo and white sneakers popped up on the screen and said in a high, squeaky voice. "Searching! Please be patient!" He wandered around the computer screen with a magnifying glass held to his eye.

"How cute." Julie watched the little guy leave tiny purple footprints for a minute or so until her mother said it might take a while. Julie thought that now would be the perfect time for one of the hundred questions she wanted to ask. She had noticed that if she asked something about QPID during normal conversation, her mother was less likely to change the subject or respond with something like "Not our business" or "Don't ask!"

"How on earth did you manage to do all this before computers, Mom? I mean, QPID stuff." Julie hoped she sounded casual enough.

"Wow," her mother replied, shaking her head. "That's a long story. When I first joined, assignments came in the mail in large envelopes or even boxes. Usually the names of the clients came with lots and lots of information. Most of it was useless but it was clear that QPID tried to anticipate what would be needed." Her mother laughed at the memories. "Of course, you never knew what you needed until you started and if you wanted more information, you had to ask the old-fashioned way, by mail! You'd mail a question and sometimes wait weeks for a reply."

Julie held her breath. This was the most her mother had ever told her.

"Of course," her mother went on, "most of that is from your grandmother's time and she had to deal with that for a lot longer than I did. Shortly after I began taking on clients, computers started to be used. Although we didn't have a home computer at first, we were able to secretly use special computers in certain places like public libraries or even some offices. We'd get a list of which computers were used for QPID and we would have to go to one of them in order to get our assignments or ask questions. Since this was before modems or the Internet, we would go into special files, input a question or report and check back later for a response. When home computers became common it was much easier. Then came e-mail and the Web which made us all quickly forget the 'old days'!"

Julie was wide-eyed and a bit light-headed from holding her breath. Her mind seethed with questions: *Do you still have a computer list? Can you still use those computers? Do you still have any of the old-fashioned packages? How did* ... But before Julie could settle on a question to ask, her mother's laptop gave a small ping.

The computer pinged again and her mother shook herself out of her memories and turned to the screen. Julie desperately wanted to find out more, but instead squashed her questions so she could see what the computer had to say.

She read the words on the screen out loud. "'October eighteenth will be the first day Susan Fox attends Eastern Junior High School.' Wow, thanks!"

"You're welcome," said the tiny man. Then he bowed

gracefully and disappeared in a cloudy puff.

"My first Benefit! And it works!"

"Actually," her mother said, "That's not your first. It's the second or maybe even third."

"Huh?" Julie asked brilliantly.

"Your first Benefit consists of all the information in each file, such as Susan being at the soccer game and mall and things like that."

"Ok, what's the second?"

"I'm not sure if you have it but it has to do with knowing things."

Goosebumps raised on her arms as she remembered her fear of the white car. "Knowing what things?" she asked, guardedly.

"For example, I am willing to bet that you are finding homework a little easier this year. Am I right?"

"Yeah! I was thinking about that just yesterday. In fact, I was done with my math in only half an hour." Not that she was complaining! It made finding time for QPID much easier.

"See, quite an improvement." Her mother tapped her on the head. "That's part of the knowledge. It helps you know things that in turn help you with your assignments."

Julie considered this and decided to ask her mother about other *knowing*, like the car. "What about…"

"Mom, I can't find my bike helmet!" Stuart yelled

down the hall.

"Just a minute, I'm coming," answered her mother. She turned back to Julie. "We'll talk later."

Julie nodded, but never did remember to ask about the car.

Chapter Sixteen

Now all Julie needed to do was wait. The date was a week away so she decided to concentrate on school and her friends. She wasn't about to let her secrets with QPID mess things up again. She joined the swim team and aced her first math test. Mrs. Moon was so delighted with Julie's latest English essay that she read it to the whole class. Mr. Vallance turned his negative attention to two students who had failed the last two quizzes. On Wednesday, Julie went to two different soccer games, Stuart's and Brenna's. Thursday after school the four girls went bike riding through the park and Saturday was the first horse show of the season. Julie took home a fourth-place ribbon in the Walk-Trot class while Carrie won three firsts and one second in her Jumping events. Life was hectic but good and before she realized it, the week was over.

On Monday, when Susan was supposed to arrive, Julie

was excited. Her assignment would be finished soon! She figured all she would need to do is meet one of her clients at school, perhaps during lunch, and then "run into" the other. But, again, not as easy as it sounded.

That Monday went by with Julie never even seeing Susan. Tuesday, she only caught a glimpse of Tammy dashing to cheerleading practice after school. She managed to spot Susan at a distance Wednesday at lunch but had learned that morning that Tammy was sick. Carrie was with Julie all day on Thursday, begging for help studying for a Spanish test. Julie was actually talking to Tammy on Friday when she noticed Susan duck into a classroom, but the bell rang and she had to rush to class.

She gritted her teeth in frustration. Her mother had made it look so easy, arranging a meeting in two days. This assignment was going on three months!

When she said as much to her mother, she was reassured.

"I've been doing this for over twenty-five years," was her amused reply. "I once needed nine months just to meet one person, and that was with help!"

So Julie decided she needed to come up with a better plan than "just running into" her clients. That weekend, determined to finish this assignment, she accessed all the information she could find on both girls. By eight o'clock Sunday night she was eyesore and tired, but she was ready.

Monday, on the way to lunch, Julie suddenly halted and dug through her backpack. "Oh, man!"

"What's wrong?" asked Carrie.

"I think I left my book in the classroom." She groaned. "I need that book for homework tonight."

"I'll go back with you," Carrie said.

"No, you go on ahead and save me a seat. I'll be as quick as I can."

Julie ran back to the room as fast as she could and caught Mrs. Moon just leaving.

"I forgot my book. Can I get it, please?" she asked.

"Sure," said Mrs. Moon. Julie knew exactly where it was since she'd left it on purpose. She reached under the bookshelf next to her seat. "Thanks," she said to the teacher and hurried away. She didn't go straight to the cafeteria but to the benches in front of the library. There was Susan with her lunch bag, reading.

"Susan?" Julie said, trying not to appear out of breath.

Susan looked up, nearly dropping the apple she was eating.

"It's me, Julie, from the mall. You did come to our school after all!"

"Yes, just last week."

"Why didn't you call?" Julie asked, then instantly regretted it when Susan looked away, cheeks turning pink.

"I...I lost your number, you know, in the confusion of packing and all." But Julie knew she was just too shy to call a stranger.

"So where is your new house?" Susan looked away and for a moment, Julie thought she wouldn't answer. But she did, speaking so softly, Julie could barely hear her.

"I live on Dale Lane, just east of Forty-Second Street." Suddenly she clamped her lips shut and looked down to rummage in her lunch bag. *She definitely needs a good friend*, thought Julie. But she couldn't spend any more time here without suspicion.

"It was great to see you again, Susan. 'Bye!"

When she joined Carrie in the cafeteria, she felt energized.

"What took you so long?" Carrie asked.

"I couldn't find my book right away. It got kicked under the bookshelf somehow. So how are the chicken nuggets today?"

On to the next step, she thought, mentally crossing her fingers.

After Computers and on the way to gym class, Julie "ran into" Tammy.

"Hi, Tammy."

"Hi, Julie. How's it going?" Tammy was always asking that.

"Good, but I need to ask you something," she replied.

"Okay, what's up?"

"For history class I have to write a paper on the history of anything. I thought I'd do mine on ballet. Do you have any books I could borrow?"

"Sure, I've got tons at home," Tammy said. "Fact, fiction, instruction books, you name it, I've got it. Comes from being in dance for eight years." She rolled her eyes. "Everybody thinks you need something about ballet for birthday presents! What do you need? I can bring it tomorrow."

They decided on a couple of books and Julie asked to meet her after school, if she could.

"Sure," said Tammy. "I've got cheerleading practice until four and then I have to wait until five for my mom to pick me up. How's that?"

"Perfect," said Julie. "I'll meet you in front of the school."

The plan was working!

The next day, she asked her mother to pick her up at four-fifteen. If all went as planned, her first QPID assignment would be completed by then. At exactly four o'clock, Julie waited for Tammy in front of the school, keeping a close eye on the room where she knew the Chess club would let out soon.

Tammy showed up with five books and they discussed them. They had been talking for ten minutes when Julie spotted Susan.

"Hey, Susan!" She waved when Susan looked up. "Come here, I'd like you to meet someone." She had planned those words carefully, knowing that shy Susan would have to come over, rather than be unbearably rude.

Susan slowly walked toward them, clutching her schoolbooks close to her chest. Julie introduced them and told Tammy that Susan had just moved here and lived on Dale Lane.

"Really? That's the street where I live!" Tammy exclaimed as she turned to Susan. "You must be in that house with all those gorgeous roses out front!"

Julie suddenly felt a mild electric shock run through her, from head to toe that left her dazed and covered with goose bumps. Was that what it felt like to complete an assignment? Blinking rapidly, she tried to shake off the shock and pay attention to the two girls.

"So you see," Tammy was saying, "my mother won't let me walk home alone so I have to wait an extra hour for my mom or dad to pick me up. Maybe we could walk home together, since we only live a few houses apart."

Susan nodded with the most animation that Julie had seen yet. "I'd like that," she replied.

"When my mother picks me up, I'll ask! What days do you stay after?"

Just then, Julie's mother pulled up and she said she had

to go. The other girls said goodbye and went back to comparing their schedules. When she got into the car, she finally cracked the huge grin she was feeling. Her mother looked at her and grinned back.

"A good day?" she asked.

"A great day!"

Chapter Seventeen

That night Julie felt smug and successful. Her mother had privately congratulated her and they had her favorite foods for dinner as a secret reward. She even logged on to see if she had a new assignment though her mother had said it would probably be a few weeks.

She lay in bed staring at the ceiling, thinking about Tammy and Susan. Would they get along? Would they be friends? Why exactly was it so necessary that they meet? She fell asleep with all these questions but no answers.

Julie awoke abruptly to a dark room, just like the night she got home from vacation. This time she hadn't heard any noise but she had the distinct feeling that someone else was in the room, watching her. She sat up quickly and looked around. Was that breathing she heard? She could see only shadows. Nothing moved.

"Who's there?"

No answer and no sound. Suddenly, the feeling of being watched was gone, like a door closing, and she felt a little silly. Her eyes were drawn to the nightstand and her stomach gave a tremendous lurch as she saw another rainbow envelope. A cold sweat broke out on her forehead. She scampered backwards off the bed and nearly lost her balance as she staggered to the wall switch. She turned her bedroom light on. Nobody was in the room and the door and windows were closed. She even looked under the bed and in the closet before she could breathe normally again.

Julie faced the nightstand, wondering how the card got there. Had someone actually been in the room or was it just her imagination? Should she read the card now or get her mother? No, in some way, Julie knew that if she left, the card would simply disappear again.

Wait a minute, thought Julie. She *knew* that. Maybe if she concentrated on the card, she might *know* something else. She approached the nightstand step-by-step, focusing on the envelope. It looked nearly identical to the other one, shimmering rainbow colors, but this time it had her name in metallic letters. She felt nothing threatening or dangerous. In fact, there was almost a sense of quiet excitement about it, something she couldn't put into words.

As Julie picked up the card, she realized that even

though she had been startled and nervous at the thought of someone in her room, she had felt no hostility. She quickly opened the envelope and read the message.

"Congratulations on your success, the first of many. You are going to be quite an asset to the organization. QPID
P.S. You *will* know. Have patience."

She blew a breath out, causing the paper to flutter. I will know what? The answers to all these questions? About just this assignment or about QPID in general? Even one or two answers would be enough. "Have patience." She snorted. Easy to say when you are the one sending the card! Whoever it is.

The next week, Julie discreetly watched Susan and Tammy at school. She really wanted to know why QPID brought them together. Well, with her help. Her mother had said she may never know, but she couldn't forget the card and its promise of answers.

The two new friends walked home together nearly every day after school. Their days of after-school activities matched, even though they had completely different interests. Often Julie would see them together during the school day as well, sometimes along with Tammy's other friends.

One day, Julie was changing classes when she noticed a small crowd gathered at the side of the science lab, away from the main walkway. Normally she would just ignore it but a familiar voice reached her ears and she turned back. She recognized the taunting, cruel voice as that of Mitzi Long, one of the school bullies. But how was she hearing it? That crowd was many classrooms away with lots of students milling around in their usual noisy fashion. Yet Julie could hear everything as if she were right in the middle of the crowd. She squinted and could barely see Mitzi and five girls surrounding a lone girl. Just then, she caught a flash of long blond hair on the girl in the middle. It was Susan! Julie just knew that Mitzi was bullying the shy, withdrawn girl. She began walking towards the group, watching and listening intently.

"I said I wanted to see that book, Shrimp," Mitzi said. Susan shook her head, clutching a book to her chest, tears in her eyes. There was evidently more going on than Julie had seen. "I guess I'll just have to take it, then. Beth, Rianne, make sure she stays right there while I take a look."

I have to help her, Julie thought. She walked faster but knew she couldn't get there in time. She realized that somehow, her vision and hearing were being enhanced. QPID? But for what purpose? She wouldn't be able to help!

"Mitzi!" Everybody jumped at the loud voice that came from the other side of the hallway. "What's going on?" Tammy strode into the middle of the group, eyes flashing.

"None of your business, pom pom girl," Mitzi sneered. Julie froze midstep.

"It's my business if I want it to be. We're going to be late for class, Susan. Let's go." She took Susan by the arm and quickly led her away from the group. The bullies were taken completely by surprise at this sudden boldness and hesitated just a bit too long. Tammy and Susan, walking fast, were well away before Mitzi could react. Even though it seemed to be over, Julie could still hear them talk.

"You see, Susan," Tammy was saying, "Show no fear and act confident and they will leave you alone. And if they don't, they will answer to me!"

Julie's heart hammered in her ears and she felt a smile on her face. She'd done this. She'd brought the two together so that Mitzi could no longer bully Susan. And QPID had shown her why. Was this the reason that they needed to be friends? There was no doubt in her mind that Susan had needed a friend, but perhaps she had needed a protector as well. Was that it? It didn't seem that important, but something her mother said rang in her mind.

"Even though most relationships between people your age will not last, they are important in helping shape who we are and how we get along with others." This must be what she meant. Maybe Susan would learn how to be a stronger person because of her relationship with Tammy. That felt right, and yet Julie sensed it wasn't over yet.

Deep in thought, she turned to walk to her next class

and literally bumped into someone.

"Oh, sorry." Rubbing her nose, she looked up into the frowning face of Mr. Vallance. She caught her breath. Oh, no, the one teacher she did *not* want to notice her.

"What's going on that has you so distracted, mmm... Julie Hatcher, isn't it?" he asked in a slow, lazy voice.

"N-n-nothing. Just thinking," she said, wondering if she had just doomed herself for the semester. His eyes flicked to the crowd of bullies that was now breaking up. Her heart leaped into her throat. Had he been watching her?

"I see." He gave a small nod and, with a smile that did not look the least bit pleasant, stood aside to let Julie pass. After about ten steps, she could still feel his eyes boring into her back. She risked a quick glance over her shoulder. Yes, he was still looking at her. She groaned inwardly. She had done it now.

"What in the world did you do to Mr. Vallance?" asked Carrie the next morning after History. He had glared at Julie all morning, fired off questions she couldn't have possibly known the answers to, and criticized her choice of ballet history for her paper. "I thought by now we were past the danger stage!"

"I accidentally ran into him in the hall yesterday. Headfirst!"

"Oh. Bummer," was all Carrie said.

"Nothing to do now but just endure it," Julie replied.

Privately, however, she thought Mr. Vallance was overdoing it, even with his reputation for picking on people in class. She hoped if she acted unconcerned, he would give up.

About a week later, Julie was going to swim practice after school when she caught sight of Tammy and Susan talking. She waved at them as she walked by. They waved back and continued talking.

"Just go ahead and start walking, Susan," Tammy was saying. "I'll catch up after I turn in this paper. Go on," she urged when Susan seemed to hesitate, "I'll be only a few minutes behind you."

Julie continued on to swim class, the conversation already slipping to the back of her mind. Just as she opened the door to the gym, she got that strange feeling of danger again. She looked around but saw nothing out of the ordinary. Almost against her will, she found her feet taking her back the way she came, to the front of the school. It was quite a long distance and before she realized it, she was running. Just as she reached the street, she noticed a dirty, white car disappearing down the road that Tammy and Susan took home.

With a feeling close to panic, she recognized the car as the same one she had run from all those weeks ago. But this time, Julie wasn't the one in danger. She *knew* this, just as she had been so sure before. She took off running.

This is crazy, she thought. *What can I do? I'll never get there in time. What if it turns out to be nothing and I am just losing my marbles?* But her body wasn't responding to logic, it kept on going toward the car and Susan. Suddenly she got a cramp in her leg and had to stop just as she turned onto the same street. She looked up and there was the car. Her hands flew to her mouth as she realized that it had stopped right by Susan.

Julie tried to limp along, rubbing her leg. Should she yell or something? But they were still too far away! She saw Susan abruptly turn around and start walking back to the school. Then, Julie noticed another moving figure. It was Tammy, running toward Susan, waving her arms and yelling. The car started to back up but stalled instead. By the time it had restarted, Susan was already with Tammy, heading further away from the car. It looked as if the car might make a U-turn, but whoever was driving evidently thought better of it and drove off.

Julie cheered inwardly. Disaster had been averted because the two girls were friends. QPID had been right after all, and she had helped make it happen! Now she understood why her mother had said some Benefits were more important than money. Julie felt like a million dollars!

Chapter Eighteen

Julie told her mother all about the event, excited about her part in solving the problem. Her mother, however, did not seem as thrilled.

"Why didn't you tell me about this car before?" she asked.

"I, um, just never got the chance, I guess." Julie's smile faded.

"What did the car look like? What was the license number? How many times did you see it and where?"

"Mom, it was probably nothing. Why are you getting so worked up?"

Her mother took a deep breath. "You just told me that you *knew* that the car was dangerous, both times, didn't you?"

"Yes, but I just figured it was my imagination working overtime."

"Julie," She placed her hands on her hips. "Remember our discussion about knowledge coming easier to you, why Math seems easier and sometimes you just know what to say?"

"Yes."

"This works in other things as well. If you knew that the car was dangerous, there is more than a good chance that it is. If this had happened before you were a member of QPID's team, then I would say that it might have been your imagination." Julie's mouth suddenly went dry and her heart was pounding so hard she couldn't think.

"You mean I was right?" she croaked. "I was in danger? But Susan is safe now. The danger is over."

"Over for Susan, maybe, but not for others. Now, I need you to remember the details so I can phone the police." Her mother grabbed a pencil and paper.

Julie shook her head. "But I don't know the license plate and all I know about the car is that it was a dingy white color."

"Yes, Julie, you *do* know," her mother insisted. "Close your eyes, take a deep breath and try to relax."

Julie did as she was told. She swallowed against growing nausea.

"Now," her mother said quietly. "What kind of car was it?"

"A 1998 Ford Taurus, white, but faded, with a dent above the rear passenger-side wheel." Her eyes flew open. How did she know all that? QPID again? Her mother wrote this down and nodded at Julie to close her eyes again.

"What was the license plate number?"

She thought about it but shook her head.

"You're trying too hard," her mother told her. "Just let it come."

Julie tried to think of nothing and as she began to relax, an answer popped into her head. "AVX-323."

"Good," said her mother and left to phone the police.

Two days later, her mother gave Julie the morning paper to read. On the front page was a headline that read "Anonymous tips lead police to kidnapper/bank robber." It turned out that the car was driven by a man wanted in two other states for previous crimes. His usual ploy was to kidnap a lone teenager and force them to help in robbing a bank. He would use the hostage as a shield, only letting them go when his getaway was assured. Julie read on.

"One anonymous phone call reported that a man in a white car had stopped to ask a local teen for directions. He then tried to talk the teen into getting in the car to show the way. Wisely, the teen ran off instead and called the police. Another tip later that evening reported that a strange vehicle had been spotted driving slowly around the neighborhood several times. This tip included the make of the car as well as the license plate number. The police were able to locate the suspicious vehicle and confirm the identity of the wanted man."

Julie was amazed. The first tip must have been Susan or Tammy and the second was her mother. She was right in *knowing* the danger, and shuddered to think of the close calls she and the other girls had. From now on, she would trust her instincts. Also, she promised herself to find out more about QPID. Was it a person? A company with lots of people? Grandma would be here at Christmas. Maybe she would know more.

Julie logged on but there was no assignment yet. She wondered what it would be. Would it be someone she knew? Girls or boys or both? Easier, harder? Would she get more Benefits? The first assignment had been much more difficult than she expected.

Yet, despite all the troubles of her first job, Julie couldn't wait for her second. It couldn't be any harder or more dangerous, she thought.

Or could it?

Epilogue

"Explain yourself," demanded the woman. She was an ordinary executive behind an ordinary desk in an ordinary office building of an ordinary city.

"Explain what?" asked the man. Everything about the man was also ordinary with the exception of his eyes. They had an extraordinary gleam that could best be described as youthful idealism.

"Don't try to act innocent. You know we don't usually recruit until fifteen or older."

"This is a special case," said the man.

"Don't give me that."

"She *is* special." The man hesitated then continued in a rush. "She's the one we have been looking for."

"This one?" The woman's eyebrows rose. "This, this *child* is the future of our organization?"

"I believe so."

"I suppose *It* showed that future."

"Well, only as a possibility." He tugged at his collar. "But all my instincts say she is the one."

The woman flipped through the file on the desk. "Her mother has been with us for years. Fairly successful, too."

"Her grandmother's even better but I have the feeling this one will far outstrip both of them."

"Hm." She continued perusing the file.

"Well? May I continue? She had a very successful assignment. Not an easy one either."

"She could have gotten lucky." The woman shook her head. "She's not very outgoing. Don't know if she can overcome that in the long run."

"She will." He sounded determined. The woman narrowed her eyes.

"You let her see the reason for the set-up, didn't you?"

"Well, um, yes I did." He sat up a little straighter. "There was no security breach."

"But you know that's not how we do things."

"And you know how I feel about that. It would help all our agents if we…" The woman held up a hand to cut him off.

"No more of that." She closed the file and eyed the man. She pursed her lips then slid the folder toward him. "You may continue with Julie Hatcher."

"Thank you." He tucked the file under his arm and left her office with a smile.

Look for Book two of The QPID Archives!

Julie's second assignment involves...gulp...boys! Not only is she clueless about boys, but this time she has a time limit! In attempting to introduce her two clients, she manages to alienate her brother and has to put up with a *lot* of teasing at school.